SMALL
STATIONS
FICTION

Xelís DE TORO

THE CLOWNS FROM PARADISE

Published in 2022 by
SMALL STATIONS PRESS
20 Dimitar Manov Street, 1408 Sofia, Bulgaria
You can order books and contact the publisher at
www.smallstations.com

This book was first published in the Galician language as *Os saltimbanquis no paraíso* by Sotelo Blanco Edicións (Santiago de Compostela, 1999). A list of our fiction titles can be found at www.smallstations.com/fiction

More information about the author can be found on his website www.xelisdetoro.net. The cover illustration by Jim Sanders is 'Closer to the Not-Knowing', 2013. For more examples of this artist's work, please visit his Instagram account, @sansjimsanders

La traducción de esta obra ha recibido una ayuda del Ministerio de Cultura y Deporte de España
The translation of this work has received a grant from the Spanish Ministry of Culture and Sport

ISBN 978-954-384-128-8

Xelís DE TORO

The Clowns from Paradise

WINNER OF THE SAN CLEMENTE PRIZE

Translated from Galician by John RUTHERFORD

Small Stations Press

This book began as a homage to Jim Jarmusch.

She lives with animals. Certain animals [...] I doubt whether she chose the animals she lives with; they, I guess, chose her. Which would be normal, for it is they who live in her. Inhabit her.

John Berger, *Photocopies*

1

The running girl came to a sudden halt in the chill of the morning. In her blue rubber boots, wet from splashing in the puddles on the pavement, she sidled up to a lamppost. She was staring, as tears ran down her face to her upper lip, at a man with a straggly beard and unkempt hair who was in front of her, and coming closer. A red-cheeked young woman hurried behind the girl, calling out to her in curt cries, gasping for breath. She was pushing a pram from which hung supermarket plastic bags, and every so often she raised her hand to a black felt hat balanced precariously on her head.

The little girl wiped her tears away on her coat-sleeve, and of her nervous weeping only a few feeble, quiet sobs remained. She was seeking the protection of the lamppost, clutching it with frozen fingers, never taking her eyes off the slovenly stranger limping towards her and swaying as if the plastic bags in his hands were pulling him off balance.

The mother and the man reached the girl at the same time. The mother, keeping hold of the pram, began to scold the girl, and the man walked on, directing a glance of curiosity back towards them. Glum, thumb in mouth, the girl heard her mother's yells. Every so often she looked up to make sure the man was continuing on his way. When she saw he was far off, she wriggled free of her mother and started to run again, heedless of her threats, scattering bitter tears along Stockwell Road on a cold December day.

The man walked on. Beneath his grey overcoat with its grubby elbows bulged a thick jersey of brown wool, frayed at the neck and showing at the wrists. His dirty, greasy hair looked as if much effort had been needed to comb it. In spite of his limp, his physique conveyed an air of grace and elegance. His was a debilitated body that displayed the marks of neglect, but slender and well proportioned. His overgrown, bedraggled beard and moustache framed sharp lips that muttered timid words when not sketching a slight smile.

The man walked on down Stockwell Road, numb hands gripping bag-handles. His head and shoulders were thrust forward as if to cleave the frozen air, and he ignored the people swathed in warm clothes who neared him and then stepped aside so as not to bump into him.

He stopped by the windows of a café, not letting go of his bags. After a few moments of indecision, he went in and sat by the windows. He put his bags on the table and waited to be served, without suppressing a smile that revealed more tranquillity and contentment than happiness.

Two waiters in white shirts behind the counter muttered to each other in Portuguese about this newcomer, indicating without pointing, gesturing without looking, trying to decide whether to serve him. After a while the older one made a sign of semi-approval and walked over to the coffee machine. The younger waiter remained behind the counter, opposite the table where the muffled man was rummaging through his pockets. Eventually he collected a few coins together on the table with flourishes made necessary by his tight, uncomfortable clothes. He stood up and went to the counter, eyeing the showcases that contained pastries. He addressed the waiter in English to order a *galão* and two custard tarts. After laying the coins out on the counter, he took his time to go back to his table and sit down. He rubbed his lame leg as he waited for the coffee and the tarts.

The place was twice as big as before. They'd carried out the works they were planning three months earlier when he was in here enjoying the same tarts but in conditions that were so different. Three months, that was more or less how long it was since he'd sat here with Jane. Contours of puzzlement spread over his lips as he remembered that he'd been sitting right here, here on this very spot, with Jane, eating custard tarts. He didn't doubt that this place, the tarts, Jane, formed a point that was clear, isolated, specific, precisely marked out in his memory. It was a point in a time that had gone, was in a past. But the idea of time left him deep in thought. When? How to measure that time? He mumbled 'three months', but this measure sounded so impartially real: it didn't convince him that three months provided a clear explanation of the time that had passed. He needed a measure that could explain and distinguish going from coming, a time that was dripping wet and a time that can stop. A time that's buried and eventually rises back to the surface. A time that can continue to measure what no longer exists.

He picked up a custard tart and gazed at its round, singed, creamy, sweet surface. He opened his mouth, arched his lips until they could stretch no further, and sank his teeth into it. The contact of his teeth with the custard and the puff pastry was different from how it had felt before. The sweet pastry, moving in accordance with the movements of his tongue and jaws, and the taste were sensations he hadn't experienced earlier, at that uncertain point stored away in the past. The sweetness of the tart was converted into gentle lines upon his face, and his scruffy appearance transmitted an air of well-being similar to that of a levitating angel.

2

Cars scurried down Brixton Hill like ferrets down a rabbit-hole, brushing against each other's bodywork, mudguards and wheels, elbowing each other as if the bell had just been rung in the pub and it was time to order the last pint. Vicente stopped at the traffic light by Brixton station and waited for the rivers of people entering and leaving it to go past.

The car's retractable roof was down and, although the radio was on, Vicente and Jane were at the mercy of the shouts and other noises coming and going at one of London's busiest tube stations. They heard, in rhythmic alternation, the prayers of the preachers positioned on the pavements and calling for the conversion of souls, the forsaking of sin and the extirpation of the devil within us; the cries of 'Seven lighters a pound' and 'Incense, incense'; the yells of the members of the Socialist Workers Party, 'Class brothers, brothers in the fight to save the National Health Service'; the police-car sirens that blared rapid, wounding melodies with mathematical obstinacy; and in the background that noise in constant crescendo, that human rumble, that mouth of mouths always open, emerging from the underground, climbing on to the buses, bellowing in the market.

Vicente took the opportunity to glance sideways through his dark glasses at Jane while she adjusted her make-up in a mirror that she took from her handbag. She returned a smile of half-done eyebrows and newly reddened lips. The lights switched to green and the car rolled forward, as Vicente twiddled the dial in search of Capital Radio. A little further on he turned left and entered Stockwell Road, passing the skatepark on the right and the hexagonal Baptist church on the left. Jane looked at him from time to time, leaning back in her seat, taking deep breaths, trying to smell her own perfume and avoid smelling the car fumes that on these summer days became even stickier and spread films of grime over windows. He parked up one of the side-streets and alighted to open her door. They walked back to Stockwell Road. Once there was a gap in the traffic he smoothed his hair back with both hands and indicated that she could cross. They entered the Portuguese café in front of them.

It was a small café, with little room for customers to stretch their legs. It was heavy with decoration that intensified its luminosity: mirrors, white walls and tables, glass, transparent showcases with mirrored backs and bases, reflective metal. In the middle there were three or four tables, and a white board ran the length of the window that gave on to the street; along it there were high stools where one could sit watching the bustle of the people and the cars. In this ode to luminosity there were a few scattered details that contradicted its decoration without a homeland and revealed the roots of those who ran the business and their customers: offers of flights to Alentejo, the Azores and Porto, advertisements for Portuguese photographers and musicians for weddings, vacancies in a nursery where Portuguese was spoken. The customers were mainly Portuguese, and eyes were raised at the entry of anyone who did not belong to the South London Portuguese community.

This first stretch of Stockwell Road could well be called Little Portugal. Portuguese shops and bars, Portuguese flags on restaurant doors, menus only in Portuguese, sawdust on bar floors, and always that ubiquitous moustachioed man seated at a table, with one hand clutching a glass and the other flicking the ash from a cigarette, who gazed out at the street, peered into the depths of your eyes and, always anxious to make himself useful, informed the bar owner each time a new customer arrived.

In the middle of the white, well-lit, mirrored showcase, heaped upon a dish, were the much-esteemed tarts that the Portuguese call *pastéis de nata*: thick, creamy custard, its surface singed in the oven, contained in puff pastry. They were the reason why Vicente had brought Jane to the café. He'd grown up with Portuguese custard tarts in Northwest London: they'd been the prize for good marks at school, the pudding on a birthday, and a fond offering to help him recover from the flu. He'd learnt to consider them superior to other puddings, Portuguese or not.

He went to the counter and waited to be served. The waiters were talking to some builders, also Portuguese, who were measuring the walls and discussing a future extension of the premises. He scanned, without much interest, a leaflet that announced the inauguration of London's first Portuguese-language programme, on Spectrum, the Greek radio station.

When a waiter finally came, Vicente ordered two *galões* and a plate of custard tarts. He did so in Galician, with the usual substitutions to make it sound like Portuguese. The waiter, as almost always happened in such circumstances, replied in Spanish after glaring at him with that geographical coldness from which he was trying to fathom what, or how, or from where this character who spoke such wretched Portuguese could be. Another of those attempts, almost always futile, to find some use for the way of talking that his parents had never managed to tear from their lips right up to the day they died in Willesden Green, and that had never been of much use to him. He turned back, removed his dark glasses and smiled at Jane, who was waiting for him perched on a stool.

He paid, picked up the coffees and the pastries and joined Jane where she sat with her elbows on the board that extended across the window. The men with their families at the central tables were scrutinising Jane to make sure that each of her limbs was in its proper place, as they told their children to keep quiet and eat their pastries, argued with their wives about plans for a first communion or some other family affair, or discussed details of the extension of the premises with the waiters and the builders.

Jane chattered and made grand gestures as her plaits and earrings flew about her face like the swings on merry-go-rounds in funfairs. She was a slim Afro-Caribbean woman – she'd told Vicente that her father was Dutch and her mother was from Trinidad – with fleshy lips and a radiant gaze. As she ended her sentences she arched her eyebrows, pressed her lips together and curled them forward.

While she recalled the night they'd met and agreed to meet again, Vicente kept removing and replacing his dark glasses as he listened in a distanced way, without interrupting her. In an attempt to keep the conversation alive, she told him about matters she'd already explained at their earlier meeting. She'd gone out with her friends on a hen-night. They'd happened to finish up in that pub after a good meal in a Chinese restaurant, during which they'd hired a striptease act. What they were least expecting was to find a group of jugglers in the pub. Vicente's reactions were all physical: movements of limbs and changes of position. Jane felt a little uneasy at these purely bodily responses to her words, and she was probing for a place where he could join the conversation. This was their first date, and a chance had to be made for something to happen. Vicente seemed rather too much of a poser for her taste, with his dark glasses now before his eyes, now lodged in his hair, now in his hands.

She didn't feel altogether at ease with the gallantry of this opener of doors and indicator of where she should sit and where she should walk, as if he were some traffic policeman; but that wasn't a sufficient reason for giving it all up so soon.

Nor did Vicente feel totally happy with this situation. Things weren't turning out as he'd planned, and an ineffable sense of fatality was overcoming him by the minute. It was an aesthetic fatality: the perfection he'd craved for this date on this day was fading away, and he couldn't do anything about it. Sometimes he shook such thoughts off and tried to act; but that was exactly what he was doing – acting. He was trying to play himself as he would be if he weren't beginning to feel this sense of fatality. His awareness that he was playing himself only made things worse and initiated an uncontrolled series of tense movements.

There was an explanation of why Vicente felt a certain unease but also a certain detachment in the face of this moment, as if it didn't concern him. For him, eating custard tarts with a woman was a ceremony over which he took meticulous care; it was more complex and intricate than a simple invitation to go to a pub for a drink. For Vicente, custard tarts in themselves, and the act of consuming them, had the exquisite carnal overtones of something like a devouring; it would be wrong to reduce this to a simple sexual connotation. It was the act of sweetness, cannibalism, carnal communion: the immediate relationship between the savouring of what he considered to be the jewel of Portuguese pastries and the closeness of mouths. To leap through the burning hoop of a custard tart was for him to enter the perfect circle of pleasure. Whenever he started this ceremony he wanted to conclude it, round it off, or at least leave the pathway of desire open.

This time it was different: he'd have to cut the ceremony short, and the only one responsible for this was himself. That morning, Reddy had phoned and asked him to do a job; and even though he'd already arranged the date with Jane, he'd said yes. He could have said no but he'd said yes. He never denied Reddy anything, and he could hardly explain the custard tart business in a way that he'd understand. Reddy was a big man and Vicente did little jobs for him – it was as simple as that. Reddy was basically the reason why Vicente could glance through the café window to keep an eye on a convertible, wear that cotton suit, and even pay for coffees and custard tarts. That's why he'd said yes.

Another reason for saying yes was that he was a juggler; and the only certainty for a juggler is that you can throw various objects into the air at the same time, since they then fall and, using the necessary skills, you can catch them before they're smashed to pieces on the ground. This was the only thing that never failed, and he was used to throwing objects into the air, sure of his ability to receive them back like a soft mattress and not let them slip through his fingers. He could have taken Jane somewhere else and postponed what he regarded as a ritual, but he'd already told her on the phone that they were going to eat custard tarts, and this was a way of continuing to put his skills to the test: calculating time and space, and intervening with rapid hand movements.

This time, however, he felt that the meeting with Reddy was a disagreeable coincidence, and it gave him premonitions of bad luck. It wasn't that he doubted his juggling ability; rather it was his inability to say no to Reddy that was holding him back, a witness to the ritual but not altogether a participant in it as at other times. He was trying to act in a natural way, repeating the actions of other occasions: covertly lowering his gaze to the pastries, to encourage her to pick one up; moving the plate towards her as she finished one; biting into one, then leaving the morsel in his mouth and assuming an expression of intense pleasure. But there was something forced and routine, and little ritual or passion, in everything he was doing. It was as if a spell, a piece of magic, were silently fading away and becoming an inexplicable shadow of itself. As if he'd accepted that the ceremony, for the first time, was not turning out as planned.

He hadn't yet told Jane that their date would have to end early: this, on top of his taciturnity, would help create precisely the impression he wanted to avoid. However hard he tried to break out of this vicious circle of defeatist thoughts, they kept twining together and intruding into his stilted conversation.

'Aren't you hot in that jacket?' Jane asked.

'Jacket? No, I'm fine,' he replied, jumping to his feet as if worked by a spring.

He'd have given anything to take the damned jacket off that stifling afternoon, but he was sweating buckets and there'd be stains round his armpits; so he kept it on, the jacket Reddy had given him and he'd donned with the sole aim of impressing her.

Through the window he glimpsed two lads near the convertible, leaning over to examine its dashboard; he kept them in careful view until one of them approached it more than he considered advisable. He left the café and yelled at them. The lads, their backpacks over their shoulders, started to walk away, glancing back with 'go and get lost' gestures. He made a show of running after them, and they took to their heels. This action made him feel for a moment that he had some control over events, it was a small affirmation of his personality on a hot, heavy, endless afternoon. He stayed in the street a little longer, standing with legs apart, then he hitched up his trousers and straightened his shirt-cuffs.

As he went back into the café the customers made comments about children's manners and their lack of respect. He smiled agreement and joined Jane, who was tasting the last custard tart. She was running out of words as she became aware of Vicente's strange and apparently uninterested behaviour.

'Do you want some more?' he asked in a resolute tone, making the most of his recent surge of confidence.

'No,' she replied with a slight smile, looking out through the window again, sunk in thought.

'A coffee?' Vicente insisted.

'No, thank you.'

He came back with his own coffee, sat down and gazed at its surface as he stirred it. After some moments of silence he looked up at Jane, who was trying to say something.

'After seeing you and your friends perform the other day in the pub, what I least expected was you having a car like that one.'

‘I like cars,’ Vicente replied, not very convinced by what he was saying.

It was an unintelligent reply, as he realised immediately. He sipped his coffee and thought, in a useless instant, of telling her the truth – the car wasn’t his, he’d borrowed it – but then he looked down, saw her long legs crossed on the stool, and changed his mind. He didn’t want to wreck everything. And telling her the truth was the quickest way to lose her, he rapidly reasoned.

‘Modest business deals, nothing very much: our little circus act doesn’t make a lot of money, as you saw the other day,’ Vicente continued.

He spaced his words out as much as he could between sips of coffee and glances through the window to attract Jane’s attention and give himself time to decide which of the possible versions of himself might yield the best results in this date that was turning out to be so different from how he’d foreseen.

He finished his coffee, went to pay for it, and they left. They entered the car and drove to Clapham. Brixton, Clapham, Stockwell: the triangle in which his life was led. This didn’t prevent it from sometimes spreading out into Camberwell, Streatham or Vauxhall, but not much further. South London, and not even all of it, was his patch. He’d grown up on the other side of the river, in Northwest London: Westbourne Park, Portobello Road, Willesden Lane, Notting Hill, a high-speed world where people come and go, look for work, make families and, as a final prize, a hole in an English cemetery. His acquaintances were up there, and his school friends, too; the Galician community had settled there, as had other

Spaniards, from Andalusia, Catalonia, Extremadura; they lived cheek by jowl with Latin Americans and West Indians. That was where his roots had been since coming to England as a child.

As he'd grown up he'd felt restless there. He'd begun to play with bands in pubs, first the blues with the Dirty Harries, on bass; then he'd started on juggling and other such entertainments, and being a circus performer offered no future suitable for a son of the Galician community. He felt uncomfortable, out of his element, and decided to disappear from the map and look for a place where he could breathe; and nowhere better for disappearance than the triangle in which he'd finally made his nest. Little more was left for him to do up there, since his parents' death, than going to remember everything that he was not.

He drove in silence to Clapham and, leaving the car in a side-street, they walked to the Common. They strolled along glancing at the joggers, the people walking dogs and the boys playing football, and then went to have some tea in a hippy café. As they sat on stools in the garden near children playing, Vicente felt a certain peace listening to the strange hum of Clapham Common: that mixture of silence and the murmur of a park with its geese and ducks, squirrels and barking dogs, children with kites, rent-boys lurking in the shadows in search of men to steal their hearts and their money, and those lush trees that allow between their leaves a glimpse of red buses, cars and motorbikes speeding from one side of London to the other. Clapham Common turns its back on its surroundings, a little piece of stillness encircled and crossed by roads that lead to diverse places. Clapham Common lets you dream that you are and are not in South London: Clapham Common, with its hippies who have built their hut in the middle of it and resemble those little stone gnomes painted in bright colours to be found in so many English gardens.

As he gazed into the distance and surveyed the Common's silent, slow-motion activity, Vicente trickled words out in the form of an excuse. Words that dribbled away from his mouth into Jane's ears. Words that explained why their date would have to be cut short. She didn't give the matter much importance, and with a smile she rested her hand upon his.

This sudden first physical contact increased his confusion. He was tempted to continue along that pathway, but he shrank back from it. He removed his dark glasses as if to convince himself with this action that he wasn't suffering from paralysis. But his signs of indecision were accumulating and making him seem like a gull at the edge of the sea, buffeted by the waves and the wind, struggling to stand up and take off.

One of his worries that afternoon had been how to tell her that they'd have to part sooner than planned, and he'd ended up turning it into a serious matter when it was nothing of the sort. The fact was that for him any first date was truly important, it really was a ceremony, although he didn't know how to explain this to her. His ritual lay in pieces at his feet and he felt foolish, like a little boy who's been prevented from playing his favourite game. Clumsy with words, indecisive, he longed to disappear as soon as possible and never call her again.

They strolled about the Common and then Vicente drove her home, to Streatham. They didn't talk much on the way. She was busy listening to the radio, far from the whirlpool muddying Vicente's thoughts. They promised to meet again some day soon, and she blew him a kiss as she crossed the road. Once she was out of sight he pounded the steering-wheel with both hands and moved off.

He had to go to Camberwell, but he decided to avoid Brixton even though this was the shortest route. He didn't want to keep going through the centre of Brixton, to be caught on the police video camera there. He drove round Brockwell Park, through little Herne Hill and on to Camberwell. He gripped the steering-wheel tight and every so often raised his hands to his head and called himself stupid. He tugged his jacket off as he drove and flung it on to the seat that Jane had occupied. Despite having left her, he still felt the unease that had accompanied him all afternoon and now made him keep slapping the dashboard.

The Camberwell traffic was sluggish, and it gave time for the homeless, tins in hands, to pace between the cars muttering and sniggering. Others sat on the benches in the Green, drinking from litre bottles. Vicente drove into the street that goes to Peckham and turned right towards a workshop whose entrance grille was open. As he drove in, a chubby bald man with muscular arms covered in tattoos appeared at the door. He looked Vicente up and down without moving his twisted mouth.

'Engine?' the man asked with a grin.

Vicente handed him the keys without a reply, and threw his jacket over his shoulder as he left.

The man dangled the keys between his fat, greasy fingers and watched Vicente walk under the grille into the street.

He continued listlessly towards the centre of Camberwell. His meeting with Jane still seethed in his brain, and he cursed himself for his clumsiness. His gaze was caught by bright colours in a window, and he saw that it was a Latin American restaurant.

He went in for a coffee. He had half an hour to while away before he returned for the car. A waiter was getting the room ready for the evening meal, arranging the tables as he talked at the top of his voice to someone in the kitchen. A milonga was playing on the loudspeakers. Vicente leant on the bar and ran his eyes over the earthenware dishes of food lined up along it, propped up to face the public: *tortas*, avocado, *mojo picón*, plantains... When the waiter saw him, he walked to the bar drawling English in his Latin American accent. On realising that Vicente was Spanish he stayed there, arms crossed, for a chat: at night, when they closed, they sometimes organised dances, and plenty of girls came for the Latin American hip-movements...

'... if you catch my meaning,' the waiter added with a chuckle. 'You must drop in – there's a really good atmosphere.'

Vicente nodded at the waiter's words without saying much. When the waiter saw that the Spaniard wasn't very interested in the conversation, he charged him for his coffee and went away to continue arranging the room. Vicente stayed there on a high stool, rolling a cigarette, uncertain which side to sit on, where to face, where to be. There are days like that. He didn't want to be unpleasant to the waiter and felt grateful for his willingness to talk to him. But there was nothing to be done about it: something inside him wasn't working as it should.

He returned to the workshop to collect the car. Rather than drive through Brixton he went via Elephant and Castle. He hated the roundabouts there, and the tunnels. He hated the pink shopping centre even more, and tried to avoid the place whenever he could, but this was the quickest way to Kennington without going through Brixton and the damned police video camera up there on high. In a car, Elephant and Castle was unpleasant enough, with its succession of three roundabouts, but on foot it was a nightmare: underground passages crossed each other and, however much the exits were signposted with numbers and arrows, it was easy to end up emerging at some corner of the square and having to keep going back down again and up again until you came across the place you were looking for.

Vicente didn't ask Reddy any questions about the jobs he gave him: ask no questions, hear no lies. Reddy treated him well, he let him use the car and paid him good money for the jobs. Their friendship and collaboration had started years earlier: they'd met when, both on the dole, they'd been made to take a course on how to write a CV that would help them find work. It was one of those useless courses where everyone, from the instructors to all those forced to take them, knew that nobody there was interested in finding work. Many wanted to stay on the dole while they looked around for jobs to do on the quiet. Reddy and Vicente more than anyone else. Those were different times: when the sessions ended, Reddy and Vicente went to the Lantern for a pint of Guinness, and more if the chance presented itself. Even then, Reddy had his little sidelines, but later he'd done very well for himself and moved up to another level. He'd begun to own cars, dress like a man of means and no longer need the pittance of the dole, but that didn't stop them meeting from time to time, as if this were the comradeship of the old days.

The Irishman wasn't good-looking or elegant, but he wore expensive suits and shoes. How he'd acquired the nickname of Reddy was a mystery, because his hair was grey and curly, though he seemed to want to deny this fact and combed it as if it were straight, with a central parting, extending it as far as he could with the aid of water or gel until, inevitably, the tips took their stubborn upwards turn. Reddy was a man of few words. Asking him a question was like disturbing an aura of silence and breaking an unwritten rule. Vicente's respect for that silence was, without doubt, one of the reasons why their relationship lasted.

The silent Irishman had acquired a good Victorian house in Kennington with a garage, and two cars that he often changed. He made occasional trips to Ireland, but it was clear that in London he'd found a way of life he didn't intend to relinquish.

Vicente stopped the car in front of the house and got out to open the garage door. He drove in, closed it and walked over to the house. He rang the bell. A plump woman with pebble glasses opened the door. She wore a tight pink skirt that accentuated bulging buttocks; she had a weary air but a meek smile. Swaying over shoes with tall, slender heels, she led him into the sitting-room.

The Irishman was seated in front of the television set. The room was spacious and high-ceilinged, but even so the air was stagnant and heavy, with a pervasive smell of cannabis and beer. On the low table before Reddy there were plates with remains of food on them. The woman went to another table beside the window and continued ironing, a task she had, it seemed, interrupted to open the door.

There was something about Reddy's women that never failed to amaze Vicente. It was a subject they'd never discussed, like so many others. Ever since Reddy had come up in the world, he'd adorned himself with a certain Mafioso style: obsessed with cars, his house, drink, drugs and his business deals, and spending his money on ridiculous things so long as they recalled the gleam of gold, silver or precious stones.

And yet, as if there were just one detail that had escaped his attention – his women. It was a mystery where he found them, how he chose them, what relationship he had with them. They were always types that didn't fit in with his air of a minor Mafioso. They seemed more like distant relatives he'd just taken out of a convent and spent a couple of hours training for a high-speed life of luxury and perdition, than lovers who surrendered themselves in sexual explosion and provided him with unforgettable nights of lust. Vicente found this detail almost touching, like his dampened hair, parted in the middle and plastered down on to his skull.

Without looking away from the television, where various commentators were discussing two boxers about to fight, Reddy extended an arm towards Vicente and, after a pause, waggled podgy fingers swathed in gold rings to indicate that he could approach. Vicente sat beside Reddy, who draped an arm over his shoulders.

'O'Neill, the explosive Irishman.' Reddy looked down at the table and muttered, 'Does this man not drink?'

The woman, all meekness and stretching her scarlet lips into a tender smile, placed her iron upon the table and tottered into the kitchen, exaggerating the oscillations of her ample hips. She soon returned with two cans of beer that she put on Reddy's low table, revealing large maternal breasts beneath her ample neckline. The men opened the cans and drank.

'All well?' said Reddy, moving an open hand towards Vicente.

'All well,' Vicente replied as he felt in his trouser pocket for the car keys and left them in Reddy's palm.

Reddy rose to his feet and ambled off towards the garage. Vicente, stretched out on the sofa, continued watching the television while the woman continued ironing. Every so often she sent him a sidelong glance as she folded the clothes. She was magnifying her movements, as if she wished to be noticed. Vicente thought she was trying to show herself to be indispensable; and he knew that Reddy had already dispensed with many other women.

'I'm Rita,' she said in an Irish accent.

‘A pretty name,’ Vicente replied without paying much attention, loath to invest much effort in being agreeable to a person who, he assumed, wouldn’t last long in Reddy’s house. ‘I’m Vicente,’ he said, in the end.

‘Italian?’ she asked.

‘Spanish,’ said Vicente, taking a swig of beer and looking up at Reddy as he came through the door.

Since Vicente had first known him, the Irishman hadn’t stopped putting on weight and covering his belly with ever gaudier shirts. Their colours brightened at the same rate as his rings and his gilt belt-buckles. He sat beside Vicente and placed a hand on his shoulder.

‘Still in that squat?’

A report about the Irish boxer started and, giving Vicente no time to answer, Reddy gestured towards the television.

They fixed their gazes on the white body, the well-defined muscles, the wet face, the hair from which drops of sweat ran, the legs dancing about the ring and the arm raised to salute the fans. In the background, cries of spectators hungry for blood and fury rang out.

The Irishman’s arm weighed on Vicente’s shoulder. He didn’t dare criticise Reddy in any way, but a silent feeling was blaming this man for the failure of his date with Jane. It was blaming Reddy, or what Reddy had made of him, or what he’d allowed Reddy to do. It troubled him that Reddy could summon him at any moment and assume he’d come, abandoning whatever he was doing to consent to whatever he was required to do. He knew it was his own fault. He was the one who didn’t say no. It was a submissiveness that had gradually grown with the jobs Reddy gave him and he carried out efficiently. If things went well for his group of entertainers and they began to make money, he wouldn't need to do these jobs. He didn't want to do them, and he didn't want to do without them. The money helped to pay for material and had financed more than one of his bad habits. All the members of the group, as well as drawing the dole, tried to lay their hands on a few pounds in other ways: doing small jobs, running up debts. They worked as jugglers and they lived as jugglers.

'The suit,' Reddy said to the woman.

The woman, meek and never shedding that indulgent smile, appeared with a suit. She took it, well ironed, to Vicente.

He stood up holding it, uncertain whether to go to another room to change or do so right there. In the end he opted for the latter, and then took a few steps forward without anyone seeming to notice. The woman was by now snuggled up against Reddy.

'You must leave that squat, find somewhere decent to live,' said Reddy without taking his eyes off the television.

Not only did Reddy say few words, but when he did speak he hardly moved his lips. It was as if everything to do with the act of speaking and expressing himself was problematic for him. Vicente didn't know whether this was because he wanted everyone round him to struggle to understand him or because there was a slow rhythm inside him that was loath to be altered. Those who surrounded him often ended up speaking for him, as if they were dummies and he a ventriloquist. Vicente himself had done so more than once: 'Reddy says...', 'Reddy wants...'

Reddy tapped Rita's shoulder and she raised her drowsy head to gaze up at him. He pointed at the chest of drawers and, resuming her pendulous gait, she went to fetch a gilt tin, which she handed him. Then she snuggled up to him on the sofa again, like a cat. He opened the tin and pulled out a bundle of banknotes. He counted two hundred pounds and handed them to Vicente, who slipped them into a jacket pocket and stood up to go.

'I'll think of something to remove you from that squat,' said Reddy.

When Vicente left, he decided to walk to the squat rather than catch a bus: it was only half an hour away, and the long summer days were an invitation to enjoy the light. He dawdled along inspecting the shop windows. He had a feeling of emptiness. Even though he had an extra two hundred pounds, he knew that this money was in his hands on its way to others: it was needed to complete the repayment of a debt. He wanted to do so as soon as possible, because he'd heard a few days earlier that the men who'd lent him it had broken someone's leg for not paying up.

He reached the squat almost unawares, and went to his room. Then he went to the kitchen with a bag of cans of beer he'd bought on the way. There were plates on the table, and an ashtray full of cigarette ends. He was surprised that his housemates weren't there, and thought they must be in the pub. As he put the beer into the fridge, he heard voices in the garden. He went over to the window and saw Andy in the apple tree. Patrick and the Lizard were beneath him, leaning on the trunk and peering upwards. They greeted Vicente.

'What are you doing up there?' he asked Andy from the window.

Andy swivelled round in surprise, holding on to the branches.

'Retrieving one of these damned clubs,' he said. 'We were practising three-man juggling, and when you least expect it... well, as you can see...'

3

It was one of those hot nights that retard movements, swell bodies and stupefy birds. The squat's kitchen windows were open. The walls were coated with smoke stains and cuttings from newspapers and magazines, principally naked women with vacant eyes. On the pipes descending to the sink, by a window, a cord had been tied; it extended out to a bough of the apple tree in the garden, and clothes were drying on it. The four card-players, Vicente, Patrick, Andy and the Lizard, sat round the table in vests, legs apart, wiping away the sweat that dripped from their foreheads. They were playing poker, betting with the greasy potato chips that each had before him in a paper wrapper.

'Any progress with the girl?' the Lizard shot out, directing the question at Vicente without looking at him as he pressed his cards to his chin, where their edges were brushed by his stubble. 'Have the custard tarts taken effect yet?' he continued in his cutting voice.

He lowered his grin as he slid his chair back from the table and watched Vicente out of the corner of an eye. The Lizard had a sharp face, curved like a crescent moon, and when he smiled he resembled the pictures of witches in story books about Snow White. The others made fun of his malign features, but he was sure to squeeze the most out of any performance before an audience of children. In one of his many disguises he appeared in a black tunic, holding a broom, and threw painted apples to Vicente and Andy, who pretended to eat them and then tossed them into the air amidst the children's cries of 'Don't eat them, they're poisoned.' When they performed, the Lizard's job was to warm the atmosphere, enliven the audience, portray characters and play tricks and pranks while the two principal jugglers, Vicente and Andy, prepared their props. He slipped out of one character into another in an instant without allowing the audience a moment of relaxation, and that is why his companions had nicknamed him the Lizard: because of his ability to shed his scales and emerge into a different life. In their most complete act, their main number, the Lizard was Harlequin. He took his Harlequin mask – voracious, mischievous, cunning, clownish – to extremes of malice and mockery, inducing the chortles of the children and the misfortunes of poor Pierrot, played by Vicente with a white face and the eternal black tear running down his cheek. These were two characters that had grown in parallel. Malignant Harlequin and dreamy Pierrot: Harlequin, the voice of the belly and of earthly trickery, and Pierrot, the platonic lover of the moon. United in their desire for the unattainable Columbine.

They had begun to play *commedia dell'arte* characters when Andy joined the group. His job was to give the performances shape and spirit, and he had succeeded in transforming separate acts of juggling and acrobatics into a more coherent whole of characters, actions and dialogues. But several members of the group had left, among them the actress who played Columbine, and this meant they could only take on small performances in which they made use of the scenes that remained.

'Don't try and distract me when you're about to make a bluff,' Vicente said, and put his cards face down on the table without hiding his annoyance.

'It was only a question,' the Lizard retorted as he peeled the straps of his vest from his shoulders, white, damp, shiny with sweat.

'I'll see you and raise two chips,' said Vicente, taking them from his wrapper. He spoke listlessly, a toothpick in his mouth.

Andy sat thinking for a moment. He was the tallest and slimmest member of the group. He had long hair, normally gathered into a ponytail. He was the group's ideas man and plot deviser. He wrote the scripts round which the improvised dialogues fluctuated, and was responsible for the innovations and other changes introduced into their performances. He laid his cards on the table face down. He remained silent a moment longer, eyes closed and lips moving as if making secret calculations. He was, like Vicente, a juggler, but he also did contortions, and balancing on poles and chairs.

'I fold,' he muttered.

It was Patrick's turn. He was rocking on the back legs of his chair. The fleshiest and slowest of the four. A happy black man. He didn't need the others' agility: his job was to set the tempo for them, a secret, slow humming beat while they were busy hurling their clubs and balls into the air and balancing their bodies in impossible equilibrium. Surrounded by his drums, he created a background sonority, and only at the end of the performances did his actions seem to match his companions' juggling skills, when he rose to his feet with drums of various sizes suspended round his body. At such moments, while the others put all their efforts into stunts that they proclaimed to be more and more difficult, he redoubled his percussive rhythms until he collapsed from exhaustion.

'I fold, too,' he said, putting his cards on the table and eating one of his chips.

The Lizard grinned at those who'd left the game and directed a sly look at Vicente while he rocked his head from side to side as if to weigh up his decision. His body, sinewy and energetic, contrasted with those of the others, who only moved as much as was necessary to wipe their sweat away.

'I match you and raise ten chips.'

Vicente looked at the chips left in his wrapper and counted them: there were twelve, the Lizard had a few more. If he matched the Lizard's bet he'd have two left, then they'd show their cards – and that wasn't how he was playing this hand. He'd hoped they'd all fold. He was bluffing, he only had three of a kind; but perhaps the Lizard was bluffing even more.

These two had made careful studies of each other's play: the way they held their cards, their gazes into space and at the others, their breathing, their gestures. Patrick and Andy were transparent: when they held good cards they couldn't conceal involuntary movements that indicated this fact. But the Lizard didn't do this, his movements kept changing and were hard to relate with the cards he held. His play often disconcerted Vicente. After a while, Vicente picked up his cards and returned them to the pack. The Lizard retained his own cards a little longer and manifested the happiness of victory in a tight-lipped grin. He slid them into the pack so that nobody could see them, as if concluding one of the tricks in his performances.

'Now I suppose you'll say it was because I distracted you with that comment I made,' he observed as he collected the pot of chips.

'Stop going on about it, will you?'

'You two might give up playing Harlequin and Pierrot when you're off-stage,' Patrick commented. 'You don't need to be fighting over Columbine now, or running away from the Captain.'

Vicente eyed the others with a frown, pushed his chair back from the table, and crossed his arms in annoyance. He went over to the fridge for a can of beer and sat down again.

They played several more rounds in silence. The chips passed from hand to hand, and greasy fingers stained the cards. Once one of them had acquired a good pile of chips, he went to warm them up in the oven and, after pouring ketchup on top, returned to the table.

'Are we going to look for new actors?' Andy asked in an attempt to break the silence.

At first nobody replied. They all continued to concentrate on their cards.

'We'll have to look for someone, we need a Columbine at least,' Vicente said finally.

'For our summer performances we four are quite enough,' the Lizard replied.

Patrick dealt another hand and, as he did so, addressed the others one by one, dropping the words in time with the cards.

'If the group is to be complete by winter, we should start to look right now.'

'There are hardly any chips left,' said Andy, wiping the sweat from his forehead with the back of his wrist.

'I'll go for more, I need fresh air,' Vicente replied.

He stood without another word and set off towards the Turkish takeaways opposite Stockwell station. They were a fair distance off, further than the fish and chips shop, but their portions were more generous. And he wanted to stretch his legs, feel space round him.

He sauntered along, examining the huge murals he kept coming across. Some were on external walls, others on party walls exposed by demolition. Some had been painted by new hippies probably living in one of the many squats in the Stockwell area, although things were changing: the Council was getting tough and forcing squatters out into other districts. Others had, no doubt, been painted by one of those part-religious, part-communal groups that sprang up like mushrooms under the protection of churches that were always in search of new followers. But all the murals coincided in presenting paradisiacal scenes: lakes with people swimming in peace and harmony, suns, rainbows, and even the fishes gave happy leaps in wonderful waters. Vicente wondered why people had come to Stockwell, precisely, to paint them. They were, like the Portuguese café, little splashes of light and colour in what was a neighbourhood in a mess, one that could hardly support itself.

Even though he was no longer vexed with the Lizard, he did feel uncomfortable with his comments about Jane. Not so much because they concerned them, rather because they were a reminder of the disaster of that first date. They'd met a few times since, but the failure of the first date had conditioned the later ones. It seemed that once the ritual had gone wrong, as it had, the subsequent steps could lead nowhere. Neither of them had dared put the last word to something that had never had a beginning. What bothered him was not so much losing Jane as finding that his methods, his ritual and above all his juggling skills were not infallible.

He saw a man cross the road in front of him, going in the same direction. He was hurrying along, with strange movements, as if adjusting his trousers or feeling an itch in some part of his body. He was young and tall, and he wore a baseball cap pulled down over his eyes; now he was stopping beside a rubbish bin, perhaps to drop something in unseen. Vicente bent down as if to tie up a shoelace, and saw the man disappear at top speed down a side-street.

Vicente strolled on and stopped beside the rubbish bin. There was something in there wrapped in newspaper, and he poked his fingers into it. It was the carcass of a roast chicken. He wiped his fingers, swore under his breath and walked away. Then he had second thoughts, went back, and again peered into the rubbish. He touched something metallic inside a paper bag, opened a hole in it and saw the barrel of a pistol. He covered it up and went on.

He hurried to a kebab shop and waited in the queue. There were five people in front of him chatting in loud Irish voices, perhaps they'd stopped off in the pub on the corner. There were always performances of folk and Celtic music in there, and it was a meeting-place for many young Irishmen who lived in the area. The smoke and heat from the griddles, the cooker and the contraption where the doner kebab meat, a mass of mutton, was turning made the poor Turks sweat. When Vicente's turn came, he asked for two portions of chips, which they put into wrappers and then into a plastic bag. His solemn appearance didn't betray all his thoughts. He picked up the chips and paid.

On the way back he walked more slowly, looking all round. An occasional car drove by, with open windows from which jungle music blasted out. He peered along the street as if expecting unexpected movements. Some of the shops were closing. The heat made everyone slower and delayed closing-time. It was ten o'clock, and in winter these small establishments that hardly survived as they tried to compete with the enormous Tesco would have shut by eight. A middle-aged Rasta in a vest was smoking in a first-floor window. When Vicente walked beneath it the man made him a slow, warm salutation.

Vicente replied with a wave and continued on his way. He knew that this man, with nothing better to do on this sultry night, would follow him with his gaze all the way along the street. He left it in the direction of Elva Road and, as he approached the rubbish bin where he'd stopped before, he slackened his pace. He opened one of the wrappers in his bag, took out a couple of chips and conveyed them to his mouth. He reached the bin and, pretending to drop something into it, brought the plastic bag up close and with a slight, nervous movement slipped the pistol into the open chip wrapper, closed it and walked away as if nothing had happened.

He reached the squat and strode up the squeaky stairs. The others were waiting in the kitchen, drinking beer and smoking. Vicente put his bag down by the sink and grabbed a beer. The others were sitting there, trying to fathom the card tricks that the Lizard was performing.

'Let's see those exquisite delicacies. Your turn to deal,' said Patrick.

'Take it easy, take it easy. In a minute,' Vicente replied calmly, as if to keep them waiting.

He put the two wrappers of chips on the table and the others began to open them and take their share. Andy sprang to his feet, throwing his chair back, and yelled:

'What the shit is this?'

Patrick finished opening the wrapper at which Andy was pointing, and the pistol was revealed to all, smeared with oil from the chips.

'What the shit is this?' said Patrick.

4

'I'm the man that's gonna make you use that gun.'

'…'

'Holy shit. You killed him! You fucking killed him!'

Jim Jarmusch, *Mystery Train*

'Four of you for a mugging – that is not very manly,' said the shop assistant in the off-licence, a bulky Sikh with a large nose and a beard tied back in thick strands. He wore a blue turban that made him even bigger. He stood behind the till, taking a step first in one direction and then in the other as if searching for a way to escape or to throw himself on to his attackers.

'Shut up and don't budge,' Vicente yelled, his face covered by a balaclava, and clutching in both hands a pistol that he waved from side to side, following the shop assistant's movements.

'Four of you and a pistol. Let me guess. You also have a hand-grenade, a butcher's knife and an infantry regiment waiting outside.' The man's attempts to show himself in control of the situation were belied by the nervousness displayed on his fleshy, purple lips. He seemed to be repeating a previously rehearsed performance for confronting robbers but, now that he saw a real pistol pointed at his head, his decisiveness was like greasepaint being washed away by rain to reveal the face of a man quivering with fear.

'Don't go playing the hero. You know what we're after, so get a move on,' Vicente shouted while the others, their faces also covered, went round the shop slipping drink and food into their leather jackets.

'Let me think now. You want what I have earned in a day's work, with which I pay the mortgage on my house and provide for my family.' The shop assistant's performance, with its mixture of false courage and fear, was making Vicente impatient, because all he wanted was to get out of there.

'If you don't give us the money, your mortgage won't be much use to you and your family will have someone to mourn for,' Vicente shouted. 'Give us the sodding money, right now,' he added, pointing at the till.

'Hey, you, leave that bottle where it is,' the shop assistant said to Andy.

'Let's get this done, for fuck's sake,' the Lizard cried, making as if to rush at the counter but not moving from where he stood.

'Give us the money,' Vicente yelled again, waving the pistol.

'Don't get nervous,' said the shop assistant, hands held out in front of him to indicate that Vicente should calm down.

'The only nervous one here is you, shitting yourself with fear. Don't play for time, because time's running out for you,' Vicente added in a stammered yell.

'All right, but do not be nervous. Come on, let us begin at the beginning.'

'Stop playing for time, and open that fucking till right now.' Vicente hit some shelves from which chocolates fell to the floor.

'I don't like the way you're stroking that pistol,' said the Sikh, pointing at it.

'Get moving, for Christ's sake.'

Two loud bangs echoed round the small shop, and the four robbers saw the massive man behind the counter clap a hand to his chest, which had a red stain over it, and slump to the floor.

The other three robbers, behind Vicente, gazed at him as he stood with legs apart and arms held out before him, clutching the pistol. They had bottles in their hands. After standing there for a few seconds with open mouths, they rushed to the door, jostling each other. Vicente remained where he was, paralysed before the counter, legs still apart, arms extended, pistol clutched. Patrick ran back and grabbed him by the arm to pull him out. The off-licence was in a badly-lit side-street at some distance from the main roads; a railway bridge stood nearby, and in its hole of darkness footsteps and shouts could soon be heard receding in disorder and eventually continuing in different directions.

Half an hour later, Vicente and Andy were in the squat waiting for the others. Vicente was at the sink dousing his face, which he then covered with his hands in silence. His breathing was laboured and he was coughing.

'Don't look at me like that. I've already told you I didn't mean to shoot. The bloody thing went off by itself,' he said as he paced about the kitchen.

Andy was silent, his back turned to Vicente, leaning on a cupboard with a small glass in one hand and a bottle he'd stolen from the off-licence in the other. He turned round, still clutching the glass and the bottle. He remained silent, and every so often put the glass to his lips without making up his mind to drink. When he did manage to take a mouthful he had to force it down.

'I think it'd be better to pack our bags and go,' he said at last, avoiding reproaches. He seemed to be addressing an empty space in the room, a ghost, rather than talking to Vicente.

'That'd be best,' Vicente replied.

Andy nodded, sunk in thought. He took paper and tobacco out to roll a cigarette. His movements were deliberate and he often went back and repeated them. He seemed to be in a strange state of shock. Vicente kept approaching him and then moving away after murmuring into his ear:

'I didn't shoot.'

Andy rubbed his head and left his hand there, clutching the nape of his neck. He seemed to be in a strange trance from which he couldn't emerge; it wasn't an attack of nerves, nor was he about to explode in violence.

'You killed him, Vicente,' he muttered finally in brief, timid words.

Vicente wetted his face again in the sink and dried it on a shirt he had hanging on the clothes line that stretched from the pipes to the apple tree in the garden.

'I didn't mean to shoot.'

They heard a noise downstairs and then the front door creaked. Vicente left the kitchen and listened carefully. From the landing he saw the Lizard plodding upstairs, grim and sweaty. He made room for him; the Lizard turned sideways to squeeze past, and for an almost imperceptible moment his sullen, hurtful gaze drilled into Vicente's eyes. He entered the kitchen and pulled bottles and boxes of biscuits from his leather jacket. He grabbed a bottle of whisky and took a mouthful. He sat in a chair and swished the liquid round his mouth as he glanced at Vicente and Andy, who was still leaning on the cupboard in silence. He stretched his legs and glared at Vicente.

'Shit, I'm going to have to explain it to you one by one. I didn't mean to shoot, I didn't even realise my finger was on the trigger. Fuck it all, I didn't even know it was loaded.'

'Where's Patrick?' the Lizard cut in. 'Anyone seen him?'

'He went towards the Common,' said Vicente.

Vicente's reply gave way to a thud of the front door as it was slammed. Again he left the kitchen, peered into the shadows in the hall, and saw Patrick leaning on the banisters. He was grunting as he gasped for air, and glowering at Vicente with wide-open eyes and repressed fury. Vicente went back into the kitchen and waited for him to come up. Heavy steps sounded on the stairs, and Patrick appeared in the kitchen doorway. His round, plump face was tense and out of control, his jaw and cheeks were in ungoverned movement. He stood for a moment scowling at his companions, and then addressed Vicente in fury.

'You stupid pile of shit,' he yelled, seizing him by the throat.

Andy and the Lizard grabbed Patrick's heavy body, which seemed to have suddenly transformed fat into angry muscle; they managed to drag him off and calm him down as they pushed him against the wall.

'Fuck the day my parents came here from Jamaica. Fuck the day I got mixed up with whites. Fuck the day the whites took my ancestors out of Africa,' said Patrick as he squirmed free of the arms grasping him. 'I'm going to beat the living daylights out of you!'

'I didn't mean to shoot,' Vicente said as he smoothed his shirt down and rubbed his neck. 'It went off by itself.'

'Shut your face, you fake. How did I ever get involved with you lot?'

'Stop snivelling, we're all up to the neck in this together,' the Lizard said, and kicked at a table leg.

Vicente sat down and the others surrounded him, elbowing, jostling and swearing in fury.

‘Did anyone see any of you?’ the Lizard asked.

‘There was a drunk lying under the bridge, and I heard people coming down a side-street,’ Andy replied as he put a cigarette into his mouth, staring at the floor.

‘I ran down Tankerville Road and bumped into a woman about to catch a taxi. But we didn’t have time to see each other’s face, and anyhow I was running in the opposite direction to where we are now,’ the Lizard said.

‘There was a couple on the other side of the road walking towards the off-licence,’ Patrick said. ‘I saw them stop when we ran out. I don’t think they saw our faces. Anyone see you, Vicente?’

‘I don’t know.’ Vicente covered his face with his hands and remained like this for a while, and then for a little while longer. ‘I just don’t know, and that’s the sodding truth.’

‘This won’t be a safe place once the cops start asking about four guys, three white and one black, with a description of our clothes and all the rest. We had to go and do it on our own fucking turf! Shit, I can’t believe we were so stupid! Vicente, you’re a troublemaker, one of the worst, and on top of that you had to go and louse everything up,’ Patrick said, going for the bottle of whisky.

‘I’m telling you again – I didn’t mean to shoot,’ Vicente retorted, smoothing his wet hair back. ‘I didn’t shoot,’ he concluded in a nervous shout, jumping to his feet and punching at the air.

‘What did you do with the pistol?’ asked the Lizard.

‘Chucked it in the bin where I found it.’

'We must disappear as soon as possible. It's as if we'd left arrows all over the manor pointing to our squat. If the fuzz don't find out it was us, they're even stupider than we are,' said Patrick.

'We've got to do a Speedy Gonzales, the sooner the better,' the Lizard added. 'It'll be best if each goes his own way.'

'If you're thinking of the East End you're in trouble – they'll catch you before you've had your first pint. As soon as they discover that the guys who shot the man in the off-licence are the four idiots from the squat in Rutham Road, what do you think they'll do?' Patrick asked.

'Go to the nearest dole office for our names,' Vicente replied, after taking a swig of whisky from the open bottle.

'And then look for you in the East End, Andy in Newcastle, Vicente in Ladbroke Grove and me in Brixton,' said Patrick. 'We've got to disappear from the map, really disappear from the map.'

'What about that place in Spain where your parents left you some land? There are plenty of crooks on the run hidden away on the Costa del Sol or the Costa Brava or the Costa Fucking Fortune,' Patrick observed.

'That land isn't on the Costa del Sol, you can be sure of that, and I don't even know where it is – all I do know is that if I sold it what it fetched wouldn't even pay the airfare, which is why I've never gone there to sell it,' Vicente replied as he paced about the kitchen, aware that all looks were fastened on his back.

'Well, Jamaica's going to be tricky,' said Patrick.

'The last time I was there, I was thirteen. I don't know anything about the place... I must still have family there, and I'm not going to turn up with three fugitives from justice accused of killing a man,' Vicente added in an attempt to end the conversation.

'Forgive me for correcting you, you pile of shit – if anyone's accused of killing a man, it'll be you. It's all your fault we're in this mess. You found the bloody pistol, you talked us into staging the robbery, you shot that man. So you're going to have to do something to get us out of this mess,' Patrick yelled into Vicente's face, grabbing him by the shirt.

Vicente stayed seated, gazing at the lamp and its charred mosquitoes. He felt all eyes nailed on him, silent, accusatory, reproachful.

'How do you think we can get there?' he said, eventually.

'Where is it?'

'In the right-hand corner of Spain, I mean the left.'

'Where the hell is that?... Nobody has a map in this bloody house,' Patrick said as he looked around.

Vicente rummaged in the waste bin, pulled out a sheet of newspaper that had once wrapped chips, and laid it on the table. He looked for something to draw with, and Andy went to his room and brought pencils. Vicente drew some lines to represent the Iberian Peninsula and France.

'This is the continent,' he explained, with pencil-strokes that made the grease-stains stand for Europe.

Andy took the pencil from Vicente's hand and continued to draw: Italy, Germany and the rest of the continent as far as Russia.

'Where the fuck are we?' asked Patrick.

Vicente sketched the British Isles, marking London with a cross and Madrid and Paris with others.

'Where's Barcelona?' Patrick went on to ask.

'Where is it we're going?' asked Andy.

Vicente continued to perfect his map, inserting Portugal and Galicia. The others stood round the table with their heads bent over it, and asked still more questions.

'Where's that other lot... what are they called... like the IRA?' the Lizard asked.

Vicente went on to depict the Basque Country.

'They're here.'

'It's on the corner, there's only sea in between,' Patrick observed. 'A boat, that's what we need, a boat. If we reach Portsmouth tonight we can nick one and set off straightaway.'

'Steal a boat?' Vicente asked.

'Patrick must know how to go about it... he's worked as a mechanic on a ship,' Andy said.

'Mechanical engineer,' Patrick corroborated, clarifying the matter with some pride.

'There are trains from Waterloo, up till midnight, I think. We've got two hours,' Vicente observed.

'I'm not going. You lot can go wherever you like, but I'm not getting into a boat with you. Of that you can be sure. In the sea there are waves and, above all, there's lots of water,' said the Lizard, a bottle of whisky in one hand.

'What'll you do?'

'Disappear from the map without needing to disappear from the map for good at the bottom of the sea so the fish can tuck in and some poor sods can swallow me when they have their fish and chips.'

'I never thought this bugger was such a good shot,' Patrick said, pointing at Vicente. 'If that guy's dead, which he is, anyone they catch will be up to his neck in shit.'

'If they catch him,' the Lizard put in.

'I want to get out of here as soon as possible,' said Andy.

'We'll meet in Waterloo Station,' Vicente specified.

'What'll we do about tickets? The inspectors are in touch with the police all the time, it isn't so easy now to make yourself scarce on a train,' Patrick pointed out.

'I'll see to the tickets,' Vicente assured them. 'At a quarter to twelve we'll meet in front of the café opposite the escalator from the underground. Now it's time to disappear.' He left the kitchen.

All four went to their rooms and began to pack their bags. From under a floorboard Vicente extracted an envelope in which he kept all his important documents: his dole card, his passport, his driving-licence and his birth certificate issued by the consulate. Anyone who demanded to see his papers would have quite a few in which to confirm that he was Vicente Vidal.

'Got any money?' the Lizard asked from the doorway.

'I'll go for some. I know a man who can make me a loan.'

'I'm coming with you. I haven't even enough for the tube. I was going for my dole tomorrow, but I won't show up there now, as you'll understand.'

'All right.'

From all the rooms confused, chaotic noises could be heard of hasty hands stuffing possessions into bags. When Vicente left his room he saw Andy leaning on the corridor wall and looking at piles of suitcases and trunks that contained props used in their performances. Patrick walked past and tapped him on the shoulder to hurry him up.

Soon they were all ready to leave. Vicente and the Lizard went first, easing the front door open and peering out in both directions. Then four shadows bustled away along the ill-lit street. Vicente and the Lizard scurried down side-streets to Acre Lane, where they caught a 35 bus from Clapham that went through Brixton on its way to Kennington. They passed the ever-busy Brixton station. It was the last station on the Victoria Line, and many people alighted there to catch buses to other parts of South London.

They continued past kebab shops and Kentucky Fried Chicken places, Chinese and Indian restaurants, drinks shops, pubs with men arguing in the doorways and drunkards on the pavements outside. Vicente and the Lizard gazed absently at their patch without exchanging a word, until Vicente stood up and the Lizard did likewise. They stepped off the bus and walked towards Reddy's house. Vicente told the Lizard to wait at the crossroads by the roundabout where the road to Kennington meets others going to the centre of London. Vicente gave the Lizard the tobacco and cigarette paper he requested, and continued towards Reddy's house. The Lizard followed him with his gaze as he rolled a cigarette.

Vicente rang the doorbell and waited. Lights were on inside, so it wouldn't be long before the door was opened. After a while, having rung several times, he went into the front garden and peered through a window. The telly was on in the sitting-room and there were remains of food and drink on the table. The windows on to the front garden were open. He saw a figure moving about the room in a nightdress; it seemed to be Rita. It glided into another room like a ghost in the half-light.

He glanced into the street to see if anyone was coming, and vaulted over the gate into the back garden. He walked over the uncut lawn, and in a back room he saw Reddy in bed, drinking from a bottle and chuckling. Snuggled up against him was the woman in the white nightdress, who still seemed to be the one he'd seen the other day. He retraced his steps, and through the open window he spotted the gilt box from which Reddy had taken the money.

Without giving the matter much thought, he left his bag in the garden and sneaked in through the window, with great care not to make any noise. He heard shouts and laughs from the bedroom, and went straight for the gilt box. He opened it and saw several wads of banknotes. For a moment he wondered whether to take just one wad and hope Reddy wouldn't miss it, or take them all and allow him to know he'd been robbed. It was a brief moment during which his heart pounded and drops of sweat ran from his armpits.

He had a strange presentiment and looked up: before the bedroom door stood the woman, a glass in each hand. He felt her cold, silent gaze; she wasn't wearing her pebble glasses and he wondered whether she recognised him without them. Her lipstick was smudged, with indistinct lines by her mouth. On her face she bore the traces of sleep, sex, alcohol and drugs, and she seemed to be gazing at him from some hazy and unstable place, as from a cloud. She strolled into the kitchen and came back with the two glasses full of ice. As she emerged she slowed her steps still more, and peered at him through straggly locks. He still held the cash tin, paralysed at being caught, not knowing what to do. Reddy's voice sounded out:

'Is that ice on its way here or not?'

'Coming,' said the woman as she shouldered the door open and gazed at Vicente with a mysterious smirk on her red-smeared lips.

As soon as Vicente saw her go through the door he emerged from his daze and without another thought seized all the money and climbed out of the window while the laughter in the bedroom resumed. He grabbed his bag of belongings from the garden and ran off, his heart leaping.

He reached the roundabout and reduced speed as he approached the place where the Lizard awaited him. Vicente hadn't stopped to count the money but, in a preliminary intuitive calculation as he felt the wads of notes in his jacket pocket, he reckoned it must be about five hundred pounds.

'Did it go well?' the Lizard asked. 'You seem to be sweating.'

'Who the fuck doesn't sweat on a night like this?'

'All right, all right,' the Lizard cut in. 'Did you get the money?'

'I did – there's nothing like having friends,' Vicente replied. He took out a wad of notes and counted fifty pounds, which he gave to the Lizard.

'I shan't trouble to ask for more – if this is what you give me, I suppose it's because it's what you can give me,' the Lizard observed, questioningly.

Vicente took out another twenty-pound note and handed it over.

'We'll have more need of the money than you. In a couple of weeks I'll phone your brother at his workshop. You can leave messages with him, or a number where I can contact you.'

The Lizard saluted with two fingers to his forehead, and crossed the road. Vicente watched him get on a bus to Liverpool Street. He continued counting the money by touch, and decided to go into a pub on the way to Brixton to find out for sure how much he'd stolen.

He entered and ordered a pint of Guinness. The time he had to wait while the Irish bartender served him seemed interminable. The men playing pool, middle-aged West Indians with brilliant black skin and basketball caps over their long locks, raised their eyes to look the newcomer up and down. Once he had the pint before him, he paid and took a long swig. He wiped his mouth with the back of his hand and went to the lavatory.

He entered a cubicle and counted the wads of notes. They totalled nine hundred pounds, which with the seventy he'd given the Lizard made nearly a thousand he'd stolen from Reddy. He opened his bag and stuffed some of the money into a pair of socks. Now he had another reason to put a sea between himself and

London. He recalled that sweaty moment when the woman had peered out at him from that weary face of hers. He couldn't understand why she hadn't told Reddy that she'd found him in the sitting-room taking the money – if indeed she had seen who it was in that half-light.

He went back into the bar and finished his pint almost in one go. The pool players looked up again; the Irish barman, a toothpick in his mouth, was waiting for his glass. Vicente left the pub, hitched his trousers up and cast glances to either side. He knew there were plenty of people who'd be ready to knife him, in the mile to Brixton station, if they knew he had almost a thousand pounds on him.

He ran for a bus that took him to the station, and there he caught the tube. People in the tube were talking in loud voices, as people did at this time of night. They were going back home or off to a pub. He changed at Stockwell and continued to Waterloo. As he walked along the station passages he had the strange sensation he was being watched and followed. He went up the escalator and as his head reached the level of the railway station he saw Andy, with his backpack on, examining the timetables. Patrick was leaning on a wall, his bag beside him. They both spotted Vicente, who indicated with a gesture that he was going to buy the tickets. At this hour you could distinguish individual people's steps on the pavement. Vicente bought the tickets and, peering about suspiciously, joined the others.

'All well?' Patrick asked.

'Where's the Lizard?' Andy asked.

'I left him on a bus to Liverpool Street,' Vicente replied as he gave them their tickets. 'A train leaves in five minutes.'

They travelled separately, meeting from time to time by the toilets or in the smokers' compartment, to make sure there weren't any problems.

When they reached Portsmouth, each made his own way to the docks. In Broad Street people were queuing outside the fish and chips shops, and laughter rang out on the pavements. In the docks, vans hastened back and forth, and overalled workmen stored materials away in warehouses. The three men looked for a place where they wouldn't be noticed, and found shelter in a disused shack. They had to wait almost an hour to hear the last sounds of gates being shut and people saying goodbye before they entered cars and started engines.

In the dark of the night, criss-crossed by the light from a few street lamps, three silent figures moved towards the boats. Their steps echoed on the planks of the quay like the feet of the audience in the interval of a play in an ancient wood-floored theatre.

5

The boy was kicking a tin can along the harbour wall. From time to time it slipped into a crevice, and he prised it out with the toe of a shoe or bent down to pick it up. With his head close to the ground, he poked a scrap of wood into the crevices to see if he could find a lizard or a rock crab. This was the intermediate zone between sea and land, where lizards that lived in the scrub and the fields near the harbour wall ventured in search of insects, and rock crabs, more accustomed to the sun than other types of crab, roamed after emerging from their pools.

The boy climbed down over the boulders to see if he could spot any mullet, and stirred the seaweed with a stick to frighten gobies out; then he scrambled back up to continue kicking the tin can to the end of the harbour wall. When he reached it he sat there, armed with his stick and can, gazed at the grand new bridge and the towns and villages on the other side of the ria, and spotted sailing-boats on the horizon and a distant seaplane flying off to combat forest fires. He looked towards the mouth of the ria and saw the mussel farms, rows of great rafts ranged across it. His gaze paused on a raft that seemed to have something peculiar on it. He screwed his eyes up and shaded them with a hand. He continued to gaze like this for some time but couldn't make anything out. Then he jumped up and ran off to the nearby houses.

He entered his house to the barking of a dog, and when he ran back to the end of the harbour wall he was grasping a pair of binoculars. He put them to his eyes and saw three men leaping about on the mussel raft, waving their arms and pointing in all directions. He lowered the binoculars; his heart was thumping and urging him to do something fast. He looked through the binoculars again, and his nerves made him feel a need to wee. He wanted to be sure that what he could see was true before he went to tell Uncle León. He kept looking as he pulled his willy out. The sea breeze blew his wee back on to his trouser-legs, and he wriggled uneasily, one hand holding his willy and the other his binoculars.

He did his flies up as best he could, and ran off. When he reached the first houses he hurried along an alley until he came to a half-open barn door. Inside were a cart up against a wall, piles of firewood, and at the far end a gate that led to animal sheds. His uncle, wearing rubber gloves, stood beside a large freezer; he was taking octopuses from a large tub and sliding them into plastic bags.

'Uncle León,' René yelled, clutching the door.

'Get your breath back, lad,' said his uncle, a short, sturdy man, as he peered at the boy against the light. 'Is it the devil himself you've seen through those binoculars? Come on in, and I'll stick an octopus on your head as a hat.'

'Uncle León, three men on a mussel raft,' the boy blurted.

'You devil of a boy, calm down. Is that a reason for gasping your lungs out?' his uncle asked as he continued to bag octopuses on their way to the freezer. 'They'll be pout-fishing.'

'Not at all, Uncle León, they're begging for help with their arms in the air, jumping up and down for someone to go and rescue them,' the boy declared, as if describing a tragedy.

The uncle muttered and stood eyeing the boy, with the backs of his wrists on his hips, careful not to soil his trousers with his hands. He was brown from long hours under the sun on his boat, and his face muscles were smothered in wrinkles. He had thick, jutting, black eyebrows over deep-set eyes, small, dark and twinkly. A black, sweat-soaked tuft of hair fell over his forehead.

'René, what are you up to?'

'It's the honest truth I'm telling, cross my heart and hope to die,' said René, and he beckoned his uncle towards the harbour wall.

His uncle removed his rubber gloves and locked the barn door behind him. The boy pranced by his side like a puppy, to keep up with him. They soon reached the harbour wall, and the uncle took the binoculars and looked through them as he walked along it.

'Well I never did!' he exclaimed. 'Three men, one of them black as coal. And no sign of a boat.'

'What did I tell you, Uncle?'

They ran to the beach where their boat was anchored. The boy went to pick up the land anchor and lug it towards the sea, while his uncle hauled on the mooring rope. A little later, the boat was puffing smoke out as its old engine rumbled. Fifteen minutes after that they could clearly see the three men on the mussel raft, jumping now for joy.

León's boat approached the raft, and from a few metres away he yelled:

'What are you fishing for?'

'Our boat has sunk,' said Vicente.

'Where are you going?' León asked.

'To Trasdás, where I'm from.'

León exchanged looks of astonishment with the boy, and continued:

'Perhaps you've been a ghost up to now – I've never seen you in Trasdás.'

'I've just come from England, I'm Rufino Vidal's son.'

'Rufino's son? Bugger me! We're practically cousins.'

The three men boarded the boat, which rocked each time one of them placed a foot on it. The morning breeze was dying away, and the sun was issuing a warning. The boat chugged landwards as the recent arrivals gazed in astonishment at the ria.

'Can't those two speak?' asked León.

'They speak English,' said Vicente.

'Not a word of the real thing?' León asked.

'Not one word.'

'What'll you do about your boat? When we reach land, we can go and inform the coastguard agency, if you like.'

'No need for that. We'll sort things out ourselves.'

René, his hands behind him grasping the bow stem, looked the Englishmen up and down. His gaze kept drifting towards the black man, so different from the basketball players he saw on the telly. This one was shorter and a bit chubby, and René found it hard to imagine him gripping the basket with one hand and slipping the ball into it with the other. Andy and Patrick remained silent as they gazed at the ria and forced occasional smiles to their lips.

'Nobody's heard anything about you round here. Not for ages,' León remarked.

'I haven't been back since I was a lad. I wasn't much older than him when I left,' Vicente said, pointing at René.

'Tell him your name,' León said to René. 'This man you see here is your mother's second cousin.' Turning to Vicente he explained, 'They're in Canada.' Then, looking back at René, 'Come on, lad, has the cat got your tongue?'

René was gazing at Vicente with his head lowered, which made his fringe cover his eyes.

When they reached land they found an elderly woman awaiting them. She was dressed in mourning, with a broad-brimmed straw hat on her head and her hands on her hips, making her arms look like jug-handles. Once Uncle León had provided explanations, the old lady gave Vicente a hug. After stroking his face, she pulled out a handkerchief, wiped her tears away and exclaimed:

'You naughty lad, venturing forth on to the Lord's watery wastes like that! Go and see your uncle straightaway.'

The old woman, León and René stayed beside the harbour wall, chatting and then taking their leave of each other, while the three men walked up towards the centre of town. Vicente gazed this way and that, eyes agape, as he tried to recognise things from when he was a boy. When they reached the main square they came across a bank, where Vicente changed a few pounds; then he took his companions to a bar.

He ordered food and beer, and Patrick and Andy sat down by a window from where they could glimpse a strip of sea between tall blocks of flats. Vicente was bemused by the many buildings round the fountain square. Bars, shops, even a bank, where in his memory there was just a patch of beaten earth to which fishwives came, as well as dealers from Ribeira and a few bathers, for some tongue-wagging. Of that square nothing seemed to be left except the four-spout fountain. Vicente asked the bar owner whether Roxelio's place was still where it used to be. The man confirmed this was so, once he'd extracted from Vicente who he was, where he'd come from and what he wanted.

'Rufino's son! I remember you, greedy-guts. How you made us all worry when you disappeared on that dinghy with Señora Rosita's father! The men went out in boats and found you, lost in the fog, it could have been a disaster,' the man said, and chuckled. 'You're like a gift thrown up by the sea – you've become a man!'

Vicente left and walked towards his uncle's bar; Andy and Patrick stayed behind, waiting for the food. He went up streets that he gradually recognised. Some of the shop names rang a bell, although the shops themselves were much altered: Insua the shoe shop, Carapán the convenience shop, Isolina the variety store. But others must be new ones. Some of the faces of the many people who stopped to stare at him also seemed familiar, although he couldn't put names to them or work out which families they belonged to. When he reached the main road he saw a set of traffic lights and a zebra crossing. He saw lads with long hair and earrings walking by. He turned right and continued past a hamburger bar with tables on the pavement, and then a newspaper shop. It didn't look at all like the Trasdás he'd known.

He stopped by a display window, and what used to be Casa Roxelio, bar and general store, had been turned into a café with glass everywhere, mirrors, plastic tables and a jukebox with CDs, just like those cafés in Soho and Covent Garden where he'd never had enough money to enter. He slunk in, peering all round, and a woman of about fifty came from behind a curtain to serve him. He ordered a coffee, and when she brought it he asked for Roxelio. They dallied awhile over half-questions and half-answers as each became able, little by little, to put a name to the other.

'So you're Vicentiño – don't you recognise me? I'm your Aunty Lola. Roxelio won't be long, he's gone on some errands and he'll soon be back. You simple soul, coming like this, without a word of warning! Here he is.'

A man with a grim gaze and a trimmed moustache came in, carrying bags. He was of average height and displayed the belly of one who spends long hours next to alcohol. The woman couldn't bring herself to speak, but Roxelio realised there was something she wanted to say. He went behind the bar, put his bags down and addressed his wife.

'What's up, Lola?'

She waited with her hand by her mouth; when he approached her, she murmured 'Vicentiño' and scurried into the kitchen. Roxelio went over to Vicente and demanded:

'What's going on here?'

'I'm Vicente, Rufino's son, your nephew.'

'Rufino's son?'

Roxelio glared at Vicente; his face paled and a bright spot of colour stood out on each cheek. He turned to pour himself a glass of wine. He drank it, still facing away from Vicente, then he turned back.

'So you say you're Rufino's son – you really piss me off, as far as I'm concerned you might as well be dead. Rufino buried in the land of the English and not even a sodding phone call to tell me my brother's dead. I found that out from a neighbour and then from the lawyer who wrote to me.' His uncle's voice was becoming shriller, as if he'd lost control of his throat. 'So I couldn't even go to the funeral. Rufino's son. You're family. You weren't like this when you left here. I even changed your nappies, you wretch. It was from a neighbour I found out my brother was dead! I didn't attend my own brother's funeral!'

Vicente couldn't find any reply to the accusations being hurled at him from the face that was becoming more and more familiar. He picked up the cup of coffee before him and took a sip from it. Everything had happened so fast when his father had died. Vicente was living away from home by then, and had to go back to organise everything. His mother was in a hospital bed, out of her mind. She never even knew her husband had died. Vicente had it all seen to as quickly and cheaply as possible. A quiet burial in the Willesden Lane cemetery, his father's London friends, the sooner it was done the better. It was a long time since he'd been to Trasdás or had anything to do with the family. When his parents were alive they and the Trasdás family wrote to each other, and whenever he visited his parents they'd say something about them and their affairs, but he no longer had any direct link. He remembered that when his father died he dallied with the idea of writing a letter to Trasdás to give them the news, and could still recall rummaging among old letters that his parents kept in a box, to try to find the address. But then the lawyer said he had to contact the family in Spain, and Vicente forgot all about the letter he'd intended to write.

He hadn't worked out an excuse with which to confront this moment, because he'd never imagined that this moment was awaiting him. He hadn't thought there could be anyone who'd still remember his father's death. What he'd least expected on this journey, after stealing the boat in Portsmouth and sailing half-adrift for three days, was to find a part of his life awaiting him. A part of his life that reproached him and reminded him who he was and where he came from, and told him that he hadn't behaved as was expected of him. Vicente took out a cigarette and coughed, gazing at the floor. He smoothed his hair back with both hands and leant on the bar as he searched for something to say. His uncle was directing solemn looks at him and speaking a few words from time to time.

'You've come alone?'

'With a couple of friends. We'll stay for a while, see the land my father left me, and get some good air inside us to refresh ideas – we're artists.'

'Artists? What sort of artists?'

'Jugglers.'

'Jugglers? Circus types? Rufino's son in a circus act? You really do piss me off.'

His uncle came out from behind the bar, walked to the window and lit a cigarette. He stood there looking out and greeting people without much enthusiasm as they passed by on the pavement. Vicente sidled up to him, while the woman watched from behind the curtains.

'See where that eucalyptus wood starts?

'The one up there?'

'Not the wood on the hill, the one to the right of the church belfry. I'll take you there.'

They went out and got into a car. The traffic was heavy and they had to wait. Then Vicente's uncle switched the radio on and drove on to the main road. Vicente was surprised to observe on both sides a mixture of what he recognised and what was new to him, of what had a name and what had none. There were blocks of flats with balconies overhanging the pavements, and women in mourning seated in doorways. Vicente's uncle noticed his nephew's astonishment, but he drove with his eyes on the road, not making any comments. Vicente felt he was on two simultaneous journeys, one forward in space in the car with his uncle to the piece of land he was about to show him, the other backward in time to a childhood that now only existed in his memories.

They turned off along a side-road to the church and then up a forest track. After the church, the surface was not asphalted, and the uncle reduced speed. He stopped the car at the side of the track and lit another cigarette, offering one to Vicente.

'I can't remember the last time you were here,' said Uncle Roxelio.

'I'm not too sure, after we left for England I came a few times in the summer, but then only once more, when I was thirteen, for a few days.'

'I kept telling Rufino you should come more often. But he replied that there wasn't any way he could bring you, because you were a rebel,' the uncle said.

'You begin to live your own life, and coming here with my parents wasn't my idea of a holiday.'

'Coming to see your own people not your idea of a holiday? You'd better shut your trap, you wretch, I've heard enough,' and the uncle raised one hand to his head and slapped the steering-wheel with the other. 'You, where are you from?' he shouted in a rage. 'Holy shit. Didn't Rufino teach you where you're from? It's all his fault, not teaching you. Good old Rufino. Fucking awful Rufino. My brother.'

Vicente didn't reply. He let his uncle do the talking. He looked this way and that as he remembered the past, saw new things and sensed the presence of the sea at his back.

'Why the hell did he have to go away? Did he ever own a car like this?' And he pressed a button to adjust the headrest, turned knobs after which the air conditioner could be heard at work, and lowered and raised the electric windows. 'I own a two-storey house and the bar, as you've seen. What the hell did my brother own? Just tell me that – what the hell did my brother own? Do we have such a bad life here, for fuck's sake?'

Vicente didn't want to interrupt his uncle. He didn't feel strong enough, not even to tell him he didn't know what he was on about. The one he should say these things to was over there, buried in the land of the English as his uncle put it, with a sea in between. As an inheritance he'd left him a bit of land at the back of nowhere that nobody wanted, and the earful his uncle was unloading on to him.

His uncle got out of the car, just as his eyes were beginning to water. He lit another cigarette, his back turned to Vicente. He was gazing into the distance. It was as if he were settling old accounts, performing an act for which he had long been preparing himself and which he now, nevertheless, refused to carry through to its conclusion. He seemed to be trying to shorten a long speech he'd rehearsed a thousand times.

'Those rocks over there are all that's left of Grandfather Serafín's house. Higher up, on the way to As Encostas, there's a pine wood, where I had trees felled to pay men I told to go and clear the gorse away. I did this the first two years, but then I grew tired of it. Now nobody can get into the wood to fell trees. I've had to pay the surveyor out of my own pocket, and the land registrar too. I've kept all the papers – when you have time you can start thinking about repaying me. It isn't much, but things have to be done properly.'

'We'll sort it, just let us get settled in.'

'Where will you stay?'

'In that house over there. We'll start to fix it up.'

'But it's just a ramshackle pile of rocks.'

'We'll sort it out.'

'A commune... this really pisses me off... Rufino's son... a commune in Trasdás.'

They got back into the car, and the uncle took it downhill faster than they'd come up, skidding over the hot earth and raising dust as he drove along. When they reached the café, he again told Vicente not to forget to return the money. After lingering there for a while, uncertain of what to do, Vicente shouted goodbye to his uncle and aunt, who were conferring behind the curtains, and left.

He lit a cigarette and walked back to where his friends were waiting. On the way there he came across more than one person who pointed at him and made some comment to others. He continued to the bar. The owner was leaning on the counter, and Patrick and Andy were sitting at the table before dishes of squid and octopus they hadn't touched.

'Your friends don't seem to be all that hungry,' said the bar owner, a cloth draped over one shoulder, as he nodded towards them.

Vicente sat down, and they gazed at him and at the full plates. The bread dish was empty.

'Those things have got suckers,' said Patrick with a grimace of disgust.

'Bring them some pork loin with lots of chips, and more beer,' Vicente shouted as he started on the food they'd left.

He ate in silence for a while, and then told his friends about his reunion with his family and the state of his land and house. Andy and Patrick listened as they stared in disbelief at Vicente eating those things with suckers. When the pork and chips arrived they tucked in with great devotion, and their spirits rose.

'I knew it wasn't a good idea to come here,' said Vicente.

'It isn't as bad as all that, we aren't going to stay for ever,' said Patrick. 'Perhaps in a month or so we can go back.'

They drank coffee and smoked. As they chatted, a group of people came into the café. They were arguing in loud voices and were presumably regulars, because the bar owner served their drinks without asking what they wanted. Vicente thought he recognised the woman whose voice was loudest. She had curly hair and was dark and plump. Her deep voice rasped in her throat and overpowered the other voices. She was more or less his own age, and reminded him of a girl he'd been to school with. It was hard to distinguish people and decide whom he knew and whom he didn't know. They were like heads extracted from a tunnel of time, to which he was adding memories. But he was surprised by how much he did remember, how much still remained in the things and people. Above all their facial features, but also their postures, the way they spoke, their movements, what they said.

'There isn't time to postpone the festa,' the woman commented as she opened a calendar on the table and flicked through it. 'You can be sure of that – you can dream up any alternative except that one,' she added, and sipped grape juice. 'We've spent loads of money on publicity.'

Vicente explained to his companions what was happening, while the exchange of ideas, telephone numbers and alternatives continued at the next table. The group there heard the strangers speaking English and brought their argument to a halt to take a look at them.

'Excuse me for overhearing your conversation, but it seems you need someone to rescue a festa.'

'Perhaps we do – a group of musicians has let us down. Why do you ask?' the woman replied, turning to face the strangers.

'We aren't exactly musicians,' Vicente said, as Patrick and Andy smiled and shook their heads, even though they didn't know the precise meaning of what was being said, 'but I think we can solve this problem for you.'

The woman in charge swivelled her chair to listen to Vicente better and look at the others.

'So if you aren't exactly musicians, what are you?'

'We're jugglers.'

6

Nelo, a young fisherman of Trasdás who'd befriended the recent arrivals, was trying to juggle with three balls, with scant success. He'd hold them in one hand, take deep breaths in a few moments of concentration, and throw them into the air one by one, after which they'd fall to the ground one by one without his tense and tremulous arms being able to do anything about it. Vicente was a few yards away with his back turned, watching the rain through the wire grille over the window and taking no notice of Nelo's stubborn struggle against the force of gravity.

Both wore winter clothes and rubbed their arms and stretched their legs from time to time. It was cold in that ground-floor area with its cement floor and stone walls. An old stone hood was the last trace of what must once have been a traditional hearth. At one end of the room a clothes line had been extended, and the rest was being used for rehearsals.

This was part of a house where they were living thanks to Loló. Ever since the clowns, as they were already known in Trasdás, had rescued her festa with an improvised performance immediately after their arrival, her voice and presence had been constants in their lives. Thanks to her chats with various people, her ideas and projects, the new arrivals were making a tentative start with a few performances. Her readiness to fix things provided solutions to practical problems like eating, transport and even finding somewhere to live.

At first they'd made the most of the light of the last days of summer to start work on the house his parents had left him, and they'd lived there for a couple of weeks. They'd covered gaps with broken tiles and boards, cleared the house of gorse, brambles and bracken, and wheeled rubble back and forth, provoking the exasperation of Vicente's uncle and the curiosity of the locals, who increased the frequency of their visits to O Pardal to collect firewood or walk their dogs and so gain a clear idea of what was already being called 'The Trasdás Commune'. But when September brought the first hints of the future rains, the newcomers realised that the place was little more than a heap of boulders riddled with holes, and that their efforts were of about as much use as hammering cold iron.

So Loló asked round for somewhere else for them to live, because that dump showed no signs of becoming a house that could protect them against the winter, nor were the locals inclined to look kindly on these out-of-work Englishmen who trudged back and forth with rubble from building sites in their wheelbarrows.

After several attempts, Loló found them a house. It was close to the centre of town, by a track up to As Rozas. It belonged to two sisters, nicknamed the Carmelites, who were at loggerheads with each other. They'd inherited it. Loló persuaded them to let the Englishmen live there. With a glass of tonic wine here and some sponge cakes there, she worked her way into their affections, first one's and then the other's; and, safe in the knowledge that she was making herself responsible for everything that happened in the house, they agreed to be the artists' benefactresses, regarded henceforth with the titles she'd inserted into their heads, patronesses and philanthropists.

Each sister made occasional appearances in the house to see what was going on there and to speak ill of the other sister. But they were not malevolent women, and their agreement with the men, who chatted with them – particularly Vicente, because the other two said no more than '*si, si*' – and with Loló, who understood the workings of their inner compasses, showed signs of being a durable one.

Vicente shifted his feet away from a trickle of water that zigzagged across the floor. He and Nelo grabbed pieces of cardboard and dropped them on to the water. Vicente found some rags and lodged them in the window-frame where the water was coming in. Nelo lit a cigarette. He was a silent, ponderous lad who enjoyed the clowns' company. He often went to the rehearsals they held in that ground-floor area, and helped them shift their props about: props they'd improvised and rigged up from scraps of wood and broken furniture, which were, with the help of tools Loló lent them, gradually taking shape. Nelo also accompanied them to their performances when he didn't have to go to sea. He was, in short, their 'hold-it-for-me-here boy', as Loló put it.

'I'm not improving much,' Nelo blurted, kicking at the air.

'If you started with two balls perhaps you'd do better.'

'Seems today's not the day.'

Seeing Vicente more interested in the rain than in teaching him to juggle, Nelo tossed the balls into a corner somewhat listlessly, and made an unceremonious departure. Vicente went up to the first floor, where the kitchen and bedrooms were. He entered the kitchen and made himself some coffee. He noticed that the ocean was grey, and formidable dark clouds were hanging menacingly over the Grallas Hills, whose tops had been scarred by forest fires. He sensed the nearness of winter. He saw Nelo jumping over a ditch on his way to the main road.

Vicente whiled away time fiddling about with this and that, and then picked up his raincoat to go and look for the others. As he left the house the rain became heavier. He went back into the doorway but, after a few moments' indecision, hurried out into the downpour. People were running for refuge in the bars and pressing themselves up against the buildings. The rain was flowing in streams down the street towards the fountain square, where it was joined by streams from other streets, and all together they flowed on towards the harbour wall, although some water was lost to the drains and some formed puddles in the road. Women with scarves on their heads and holding their raincoats stretched over them as canopies hastened up and down, while in the square other people struggled to close umbrellas that had broken ribs. The rest cursed as they ran into bars where they chatted and waited for the downpour to end.

Vicente went into Cas Abelardo, the bar where they'd been on the day they were thrown up by the sea. Andy was at a table by the window, drinking coffee. Vicente ordered coffee for himself and went to sit with him, smoothing his wet hair back with both hands. Andy wore a raincoat that was too big for him. Vicente's wasn't a good fit, either: it was also loose, and one of the sleeves had a stain on it. They'd brought few garments in their flight from England, among them none for the winter; their clothes came from the members of A Virandela's old wardrobes and drawers, which Loló was emptying to dress the artists who'd emerged from the sea.

'Patrick won't be coming,' Andy said.

'Why not?'

'I dropped by the workshop where he's doing a job for them. They've got a lot on, so they asked him to go back in the afternoon.'

'We shan't rehearse, then.'

They remained silent for a while. When the rain cleared, people began to leave the bar. Its floor was covered with wet sawdust. Men near the door were buttoning their raincoats and overcoats.

'I must go, too,' said Andy.

Vicente regarded him with surprise.

'They're offering me longer hours at the Academy.'

'Have you two been bitten by the work-bug?'

'It's all money. We need money.'

'We've always got the juggling.'

Andy sat for a moment looking away from Vicente, through the window.

'What more can I say, Vicente?'

They talked for a while about the house and what needed to be done to it. Then Andy picked up a folder and got to his feet. He said goodbye and paid for the coffees. Vicente stayed in the bar and ordered another. The rains, which had suddenly reached Trasdás during the previous few days, roaring in and slamming the door behind them, brought back memories of cold feet, broken umbrellas and woollen hats pulled down over ears. Each time one of these memories came to him, it was through a different sense: sometimes it was what he heard or saw, sometimes it was a smell or a taste. As if they were awaiting him in hidden and unexpected places: the fishermen's smell of fresh sardines, the taste of Galician potatoes boiled in their skins with bay leaves, the chirruping of crickets at nightfall; the clouds, the electricity posts and the windows of the houses reflected in the puddles as he leapt along in zigzags to dodge them. Even the glow-worms – he hadn't seen a glow-worm for almost twenty years. The sense of not being here, yet being here, being where one no longer is.

It had been a frantic September that had bustled by without leaving the clowns much time to consider what they were doing in Trasdás, or what they'd come here to do, or why they'd fled here from London. Vicente had met old friends he hadn't seen since he was a boy. Some were married, had children, cars, houses, one or two were already separated; they paid for rounds of Sunday drinks, they dined out – all except a couple of them: Trepas and Migueliño, who'd ended up on drugs, and Piraña, who'd been killed in a road accident on his way home from a disco. They all asked him about his life in London, but they gradually realised that he didn't pay for Sunday drinks or dine out and lived with another two like him in a house borrowed from the Carmelites; what was more, he'd come to hobnob with those revolutionaries from A Virandela, of which that fat girl Loló was a member. They were beginning to gossip behind his back. What the hell had that Englishman come here for?

With the rehearsal cancelled, Vicente had a whole afternoon before him without anything to do. He set off towards the harbour wall, hands in pockets and gaze downcast. Avoiding the puddles along the way, he shyly greeted the locals he met. Below him he saw the choppy sea and small boats bobbing on the waves. He strolled towards the new bridge along a path that ran parallel to the beach. It was a huge bridge that connected Vilariño with Rostro and allowed the lorry drivers from Ribeira to drive direct to the port of Murás without having to take the coastal road through Argalo, Tal, Marmoeira, Taramancos, Porto Trapeiro and Trasdás, where, according to popular etymology, you're done from behind. Vicente couldn't get used to the sight of this bridge. It was like an artificial limb they'd attached to the sea. An object of a different, alien material, fitted into the ria to fulfil a function, yes, but artificial. He gazed at the bridge with its columns walking on the water. It was a line that crossed the horizon and the sea, and often pursued him into his dreams. It was still there, in the mist, when he awoke in the mornings, on fine days and rainy days.

He went over to the wrasse rocks, and on the headland he could see the ruined factory that belonged to a Catalan company. He thought he might go there one day at low tide. He strolled back by the side of the sea and contemplated the brightly coloured houses standing in a row parallel to the shoreline. The usual seaside houses with their yellow windows, their red, pink and green walls, their blue doors. All that was missing were beacon lights on the roofs to show sailors the way home.

He saw a boy on the harbour wall. As Vicente approached, the boy began to look like René, the one who'd found them stranded on the mussel raft. He was pacing from one side of the wall to the other, hurling stones, climbing down to the water's edge and playing with a flag he'd made from what the sea had thrown up.

A strong wind was blowing, and Vicente's hair fluttered in disorder. When he came close to the wall he called to the boy, but the wind blew his words back to him. He hesitated for a moment and then clambered up over the boulders to the top of the wall and stood staring at René, who eventually saw him and approached. He had a stick in his hand with an empty bleach bottle on one end, and he walked up to Vicente with the swaying gait of children who know they're being observed. He was swathed in a buttoned-up overcoat and a scarf round his neck.

'The sea'll get you if you don't watch out,' said Vicente.

'The ones it almost got were you lot. It won't get me – I know how to look after myself, I keep my wits about me,' René retorted, and twirled the bleach bottle round the tip of the stick. His voice was hoarse, he had a sore throat.

'No school today?'

'I'm poorly – can't you hear how I'm talking?' said René. Under his coat and scarf he wore many layers of clothing that made his body resemble a great bundle that ended in tiny limbs in the form of feet and hands.

'In this weather it's better to stay at home.'

'It's those buggers in Murás, sending us the rains. Look, the sky's clear over there. When they see a cloud coming they send it here, they think they're ace. Our sky's always cloudy. And their girls are prettier – great big eyes, so people say, and their tits...' he cupped his hands in front of his chest in imitation of a woman's large breasts.

'Your time for all that will come, you aren't old enough to go after girls – better go after mullet instead, quite sufficient for you. Toss them a few breadcrumbs, makes them tipsy.'

'That's just what you say – I do have a girlfriend, she's called Verónica if you don't believe me,' white-faced René replied, puffing his fringe up from his eyes. 'She's

Señor Tomás the butcher's daughter, and I've already touched her coochies, if you must know. But once I'm a grown-up I'll leave her and go to Murás. I'll spend the whole day in sunglasses on the café terraces, chatting the German girls up,' René continued defiantly, and set off for the end of the harbour wall with his stick and bleach bottle.

'Wouldn't you be better off in bed with a hot-water bottle?' Vicente shouted after the departing boy.

'I'll go home soon – just came to make an inspection.'

Vicente walked away, chuckling. He imagined René with his little mouth repeating that his dreams would all come true, wounded in his pride, tossing stones into the sea, taking revenge on a goby, pulling the legs off a rock crab.

Vicente climbed towards the main road. He passed small houses, people in doorways and furtive glances from behind half-pulled-back curtains. On he went, resolute, alone, aware of the presence of hazy, distant countenances on either side. Sharp-faced, he could hear a low rumble entering his ears, as if there were a sea inside his head; he was walking along a tunnel through the ocean as crossed eyes sprouted among the waves. It was like the aisle down the middle of the stalls in a theatre, cold and damp, with wax faces on either side scrutinising his tentative steps in the dark, waiting for something important to happen.

7

'I prefer moonlight, don't you?'
'The moon? Of course, the moon. My homeland, the moon.'

Marcel Carné, *Les Enfants du paradis*

Firecrackers exploded and there was a joyful hubbub in the arcades round the square as children flocked into it. Behind them a drum and bells could be heard, and Patrick appeared, marching down the street in a hat with one side of the brim raised pirate-style and a many-hued feather sticking out. Each quarter of his face was painted a different colour. The bells were tied to his legs and shoes, and they tinkled to the rhythm of his firm steps. He held his hands behind him, beating a drum carried on his back. He wore red trousers and a singlet with horizontal blue and white stripes. Vicente and Andy followed bearing two long poles, their ends adorned with coloured lengths of cloth that tinged the mould-stained white facades and the damp grey morning air in the square of the four-spout fountain.

Vicente was dressed as Pierrot in his loose white suit, around which flounces of wispy cloth floated, and he was swinging his free arm in time with his exuberant march. Andy, marching with him, waved from side to side the four plaits into which he had woven his long hair, and from which plastic fruit hung. He wore a bowler hat, his cheeks were crowned with red hearts, and he sported patched calf-length trousers held up with braces. A little behind them, Nelo pushed a wheelbarrow that contained the juggling props. He wore a striped suit that was too small for him, and a hat over a red wig.

When Patrick reached the fountain, the children began to clap to the rhythm of his drum, and everyone, young and old, formed a circle round him. Andy and Vicente soon arrived, positioning themselves behind Patrick and waving their festa banners so that the lengths of cloth crossed in the air. A good-sized crowd had appeared, spreading back into the arcades.

Andy and Vicente left their banners against the fountain and went to stand in front of Patrick, who began a roll on his drum. Nelo climbed the fountain, took the banners and held them, one in each hand, to form a cross in front of him. Some of the lads were pointing at him, but he wasn't flustered and kept his gaze fixed on the crossing-point of the two poles.

Vicente removed his cap and held it out, Andy hurried to his side, took his bowler hat off, put Vicente's cap on his own head and held his hat out; then Vicente went to stand behind him and performed the same operation. They rounded each other like this several times to the rhythm of the drum, played ever faster by Patrick. The audience wasn't showing much enthusiasm for this first number. The two men drew closer to Patrick. They placed themselves on either side of him, gazing at the audience, and when Patrick began another drum-roll they started to switch the three hats again, without any apparent logical order in the rotation.

Patrick stopped drumming and, with the exaggerated facial expressions of mime, tried to peer upwards, towards the top of his head, to see if he had his own hat up there; then he turned his eyes on Andy and saw he wasn't wearing it, and then at Vicente, who did have it on; Patrick grimaced in anger at the audience, which provoked the first giggles among the children. He began to play his drum again, and his companions again changed hats in apparently disordered rotation. Then he stopped playing and pulled the same faces as he searched for his hat, interrupted by the children, now more animated, who shouted 'He's got it', pointing at Andy.

After these actions had been repeated several times, Nelo leant the banners against the fountain and sat on it with feet dangling, and his hat was added to those going from head to head. This time, when Patrick stopped drumming, his hat was on Nelo's head. As Patrick glared from one head to another the children shouted 'Nelo's got it' and pointed at him: Nelo couldn't hide his embarrassment when he saw everyone grinning at him. When Patrick's glare finally settled on Nelo, he repeated his angry grimace, provoking guffaws among the children and smiles among the adults. They repeated this sequence of actions yet again, and this time when Patrick stopped drumming he was wearing his own hat; as he squinted at the others the children didn't stop yelling 'You've got it on!' In the end Patrick flaunted an enormous beam and the children shrieked with glee; he raised a hand to his hat and, beating the drum with the other, ran out into the audience, which screamed with excitement and gave way to his belled feet. The other three ran behind him with outstretched hands, trying to grab his hat, always out of their reach. People stepped aside, applauded and shouted; before they knew it they were participants in the magic of the festa. The performers returned to the middle of the square amid claps and laughs.

A few turns followed in which Vicente threw clubs into the cool air and juggled with them, first three, then four. The audience didn't stop applauding his skills. There were screams of astonishment later when Andy stretched his body in strange contortions as he pretended to try without success to climb the fountain. After this he came back down and joined Vicente in the juggling, and that was when the most widespread applause rang out and filled the square. Loló was handing out leaflets about A Virandela's chestnut-harvest festival and shouting 'This is nothing compared with what they'll do at our festa and, what's more, there'll be pipers and chestnuts – the ones you eat, I mean, not the jokes we crack.'

The light in the square became less intense and everyone looked up at the sky, suddenly packed with clouds. The clowns exchanged glances and made preparations for their last turn. Andy and Nelo climbed the fountain and tied a black cloth with white flecks representing stars to one of the poles and, while Nelo held it, Andy went down to the wheelbarrow that contained the props. Patrick shook his feet to make the bells sound in a gentle rhythm, and played a soft drum-roll. A few raindrops fell, solitary and far-spaced, but as big as pebbles. Vicente climbed up to the nocturnal backcloth held in position by Nelo on the fountain; his movements were performed in mime as he raised and lowered his legs with extreme gentleness and delicacy, opened his mouth, arched his eyebrows and moved as if he were floating in the air or tiptoeing over the softest of surfaces. When he reached the black, star-flecked cloth, he shrank back, overcome with emotion. It was difficult now to ignore the rain, falling with ever greater intensity. The audience drew back into the shelter of the arcades as the performers tried to finish their number.

The rain was washing their make-up down their faces; Vicente's was the most exposed, because his cap had no brim. Andy had a stick from which hung a string with a black and white wooden disc on one end; the white part was a half moon, its outside formed by the curve of the disc. He placed the moon at one end of the black cloth, and Vicente mimed his amazement; he inched towards it with his angelic walk, and Andy moved the moon to the other end; Vicente, with anxious gestures, tried again and again to approach the moon, which, on the string manipulated by Andy, kept returning to the opposite end.

It wasn't easy to tell whether the sorrow in the children's eyes and the murmurs on the adults' lips were caused by Pierrot's inability to catch the moon or the sad sight of Vicente's white make-up streaming down his face. Loló called out to the performers and beckoned them towards the protection of the arcades. Andy and Patrick exchanged glances and saw Vicente still standing there with mournful eyes that displayed his longing to reach the moon. Engrossed in his performance, he gave no signs of relinquishing it, and his companions stayed with him in the middle of the square.

The rain was by now pouring down pitilessly upon the performers, who bowed their heads and tried to protect themselves with their hats, all except Pierrot, who continued to mime his pursuit of the unattainable moon. His black tear had disappeared from his rain-washed face, running with make-up.

At last the edge of Vicente's hand reached the moon; since his arms were in a straight, sloping line, it rolled down them behind his neck to his other hand and, when he tried to grasp it, it rolled back. Andy let the disc run free and it continued to roll from one of Vicente's hands to the other, passing behind his neck. There was timid applause from the arcades, but everyone was anxious for the show to end and the performers to come and shelter with them. There was nothing left for Andy to do, and he hurried down from the fountain and into the arcade, while Patrick edged in the same direction until he was also sheltering there, so that only Vicente and Nelo were left out in the open. Nelo gathered up the backcloth, descended from the fountain with water dripping from him and ran, leaping over the puddles, into the arcade.

Finally Vicente, in the middle of the circle where the spectators had stood, sank to his knees; the moon was rolling up and down the U formed by his arms, which would have prompted astonishment and general applause if the audience weren't so aware of the soaking he was suffering. Nelo ran out with an umbrella and stood behind Vicente to shelter him as his performance reached its conclusion. Vicente, still kneeling, over a puddle, had one hand raised, and on its first finger the unattainable moon twirled. The spectators applauded the artist's dedication, and he paused to listen. Nelo, caught in the emotion of these final moments, twirled his open umbrella. Then they ran into the arcades, where the spectators made way for them and slapped Vicente on the back.

Bowls of steaming broth appeared from a bar, and the voice of its owner, Abelardo, was heard over the applause and congratulations: 'For the performers, poor things.' The bowls were passed overhead from hand to hand to the performers, who did their best to put them to their lips and drink despite the backslaps and handshakes. Children came and offered their assistance in future shows, and Nelo was surrounded by lads of his own age, proud to offer him cigarettes.

Vicente wiped his besmeared face with his sleeve and saw a woman leaning on a column, sending a sweet smile in his direction. He took no notice as he sipped the broth and accepted the cigarette he was being offered. Loló gave each performer a kiss and a hug, and someone held a lighter out to Vicente over people's heads. He stretched up to put the cigarette to it, and peered towards the man who'd offered him the light, to thank him; and again he caught sight of the woman who'd been gazing at him. They stood and stared at each other, but Vicente didn't recognise her; he pushed his way through the crowd and together they went over to where she'd been before, beside the column, where there was more room. The woman was holding the hand of a child of about five, scared of this clown whose face was smeared with white make-up.

'I'm sorry, but...'

'Vicentiño.'

'Yes, that's me...'

He remained silent for a moment as he gazed at her, and another smile came to her face.

'You don't recognise me...'

'Milagritos!'

She nodded and gave him a hug.

'And this is little Milagritos...' said Vicente, about to squeeze the girl's nose, but he remembered that there was nothing he'd hated more as a child and desisted, looking down at her as she cowered behind her mother. 'What a surprise! I don't know where to begin,' he added, a little nervous but happy. He was being called from the group where the others stood, but told them to wait.

'Go and join them,' said Milagritos, 'we'll meet another time. I only came to say hello,' and she waved goodbye and pulled the girl away.

The others called him again, while members of the public came up to pat him on the back and remind him of when or how they'd met him or his father. Vicente tried to respond to their greetings, but he didn't want to let Milagritos leave like that: she'd already moved a few steps away and was waving again. She'd been his neighbour and playmate when they were children. She was the dream of all the boys in the school in Argalo, who were envious because he lived next door to her. He approached her, and the little girl hid behind her mother again.

'Will you come to the chestnut festa?'

'I can't, but I'll try to come the next time you perform.'

'We haven't got any more shows yet, but I expect we'll perform again before long.'

They stood for a few moments in silence and gazed at each other, while the girl lost some of her shyness and edged out in front of her mother. Milagros opened a bag and jotted something down on a scrap of paper.

'You can phone to say when you perform, and I'll try to be there – if it's a children's show I expect Carmela will have overcome her fear by then.'

'I'll phone you,' said Vicente, and took the paper.

'Here you are,' said Milagros, and handed him a tissue, 'your make-up's all runny.'

They took their leave of each other and Vicente went back to his group, where more backslaps awaited him.

8

As Vicente peeled garlic he heard the street door open, and then steps on the stairs.

'Look what I've got here,' said Patrick, placing a small television set on the table.

Vicente gazed in surprise, first at the television and then at Patrick.

'The volume control doesn't seem to work too well, I expect dust has got into it,' Patrick continued as he plugged the set in and twiddled knobs.

'Where did you get it?' asked Vicente.

'One of the men at the workshop said he had it at home and it was never used, and I'd be doing him a favour if I took it.'

'Even though you don't understand a word of what they say.'

'True, I don't, but it's what I think he said,' Patrick replied as he continued to turn knobs in search of channels. 'We'll need an aerial.'

When Andy arrived, lunch was ready and they sat round the table. Vicente had made pasta, with a sauce of garlic and anchovies fried in olive oil. They took handfuls of grated cheese and scattered it over the pasta. The television stood near the window emitting a continuous buzz and displaying an image eaten away by white dots.

'Any of those marvellous tomatoes left?' asked Patrick.

Vicente indicated with a head movement where they were, and Patrick went to cut some up. He put them on the table and all three helped themselves.

'I've been thinking... I'm going to make a new costume,' Vicente announced.

'What's wrong with the one you have?' asked Patrick.

'The Pierrot costume doesn't work... without Harlequin.'

'Any old costume does the job,' Patrick retorted.

'Pierrot's costume isn't any old costume.'

'He's right,' Andy said to Patrick. 'Pierrot's a sad character, but without Harlequin making life impossible for him he's even sadder... something seems to be missing.'

'As far as I'm concerned, you can do whatever you like; but there are just the three of us, and all we're going to perform are separate juggling and balancing acts, so anything we can use is welcome, and Pierrot is one of the things we can use. When we performed in the square and at the chestnut festival people really enjoyed your Pierrot-and-the-moon turn,' Patrick continued.

'People might have enjoyed it, but I didn't.'

'You didn't?' Patrick queried. 'So that's why you stayed out in the rain until you'd finished, and we all got a good soaking.'

'How can I explain it? If you're dressed as Pierrot you have to be Pierrot, and I don't know how I can be Pierrot without Harlequin and Columbine.'

'Do you think that when we're in front of our audience juggling they'll wonder whether you're Pierrot or Columbine or whoever? They'll see three clowns with painted faces doing juggling, magic tricks, balancing – all they want is to laugh and have a good time.'

'I don't care what they'll see. I care what I'll see. And that'll be a Pierrot who isn't Pierrot.'

'Let's stop arguing, shall we? If Vicente doesn't feel comfortable dressed as Pierrot, fair enough. He makes another costume. I can see what he means,' Andy put in as he finished his meal.

'I can see what he means, too. Don't talk like that, as if I didn't understand,' Patrick retorted as he stood to pick up the fruit bowl and put it on the table.

They were silent for a while, sunk in thought as they peeled apples and oranges and ate them. Vicente stood up to make coffee.

'I'm talking about practical matters. A Pierrot, in this instance, is just a clown. Do you think the audience wonders who Pierrot is?' Patrick continued. 'But if it's so important to you let's leave it there – we'll work on another turn.'

Vicente stood up again when he heard the coffee maker boiling. He poured the coffee and sat down, and they began to roll cigarettes.

'What do you think of Nelo?' asked Andy.

'What do you mean?'

'He's well-behaved, and he clearly likes working with us. We're using him as a "hold-it-for-me-here boy", as Loló puts it, but perhaps we could ease him into the performances, give him something to do.'

'Not juggling,' Vicente cut in.

'He knows the language they speak here... he could act... talk to the audience,' Patrick suggested as he finished his coffee and poured himself another. 'I never thought I wouldn't miss my tea. If I'd been asked a month ago what I'd take to a desert island, I'd have said a cup of tea. And now I've got used to coffee – can you believe it?'

'I'll think of something,' Andy insisted. 'Perhaps we could put on a few scenes with themes from this part of the world. That's basically *commedia dell'arte*, the use of local subjects and languages to entertain.'

'I've already said my bit about Pierrot.'

'We can use other characters, but keep its spirit,' said Andy, defending his idea.

'So we teach Nelo to do something, he gets enthusiastic – and then we clear off.' Vicente, about to draw on his cigarette, lowered his hand. 'Come on, how long do you two think we're going to stay here?'

Andy and Patrick glanced at each other and shrugged in unison as they eyed Vicente without replying.

Vicente sat at the table smoking while his companions cleared it and washed up. Andy and Patrick went to their rooms for a brief rest. Vicente stayed in the kitchen beside the window and watched the drizzle as it spattered on the panes.

Both Andy and Patrick had arranged their own corners where they kept the objects they were acquiring. Patrick had appropriated an old sofa and placed a low table in front of it in an improvised sitting-room with walls that cried out for a coat of paint. There he kept a small radio cassette player with some cassettes, and screwdrivers and other tools he was always messing about with. In the same room, Andy had begun to put together a small library in a wardrobe. He'd placed a formica board on wooden crates to improvise a writing-desk with shelves. In there he kept papers, magazines and notebooks. But Vicente hadn't managed to sort out a space to call his own. He'd wander about the house without a set place to stop: only a small rocking-chair in the kitchen opposite the window seemed to belong to him.

Patrick and Andy had arranged with Loló to do some work on A Virandela's premises, after which they'd stay for the Galician class she gave there. They agreed that Vicente would go and fetch them after the class, and set off. Vicente saw them walk in their winter clothes along the track to the main road.

He set about killing time, whiling the hours away. He whiled the hours away as he did the days, half-heartedly. There were times when he didn't understand his housemates. What for him had been a brief escape, a temporary refuge, seemed to be rather more than that for them.

He cast his mind back over their last days in London. Their flight, the sea crossing, which had only ended well thanks to Patrick's skill. He remembered how they'd scuttled the boat by night beside the mussel raft, fearful that otherwise the authorities would be informed about it, and how they'd spent that night on the raft, fighting sleep off. He remembered Rita coming out of Reddy's bedroom – he could still feel that galloping in his chest. He remembered the shop assistant collapsing behind the counter, and his hands became clenched fists, sweaty and tremulous. He slumped into a chair in the kitchen and tried to understand the pathway down which these new thoughts were taking him. All this time he, Andy and Patrick had alluded to the murder as 'what had made them leave' or had said 'what happened happened', and had seldom made any direct reference to the murder, the fact that he'd killed a man. This was why they were there. He'd fired the pistol, even though he couldn't remember pulling the trigger. He couldn't remember squeezing his finger, yet he had an exact recollection of how the gigantic Sikh had fallen, those eyes bulging and the great bloodstain all over his chest. For a while Vicente remained in the kitchen rocking-chair, arms and legs dangling as he gazed at the wet window and the fading light, unable to do anything.

His memories of London were much clearer, better defined, than those of Trasdás, which had blurred outlines, however hard he tried to envisage them. That big face and its big nose, the shot and the sound of the body falling, were clearly engraved in his memory. He could avoid thinking too much about them, avoid accepting the fact that he'd killed a man, but when these memories did enter his mind they were tangible and real.

The only tangible, exact, defined memory he had of Trasdás was Milagros. She was like a resplendent sheen on soggy sand. A face that returned to him from the past in precise detail. He'd only seen her on the day they'd performed in the square, but she came back into his mind again and again. After the performance they'd all gone to Chucho's bar to have some food, and Loló had talked to him about Milagros: she'd had to separate from a brute of a husband, and now lived in Porto Trapeiro with her daughter. She was a graphic designer, and most of the posters and booklets published by the local councils passed through her studio. She also worked for A Virandela. Loló noticed that Vicente was interested in her, and ended with the words 'A fine woman'. The conversation moved on to other subjects, but of everything in Trasdás that they discussed, only Milagritos was of any interest to him. And now she was going to watch their performance in an English pub in Argalo. He hadn't been able to decipher her scribbles on the scrap of paper she'd given him, and he'd had to ask Loló for her phone number. Her voice had sounded friendly and calm on the telephone, and he hadn't found it difficult to adapt to that tone. It was as though they shared a code they'd invented many years earlier.

Slowly Vicente slipped his raincoat on as he tried to rid himself of the ideas that had kept him worried throughout the afternoon. They formed a train of thought that tired him physically, as if it had driven into him, battered his organs and left him weary, his muscles exhausted. He walked along, puffing down into the top of his raincoat, until he saw the lights of Chucho's bar.

A Virandela's premises stood next to it, and Chucho was a member of that association. He let them use a garage that also served as wine cellar and storeroom and provided plenty of room for their meetings and other activities. It was where classes in traditional dancing, Galician and drawing were given, and there was even a library and a cassette service. In there the problems of the town, of Galicia and of the world were discussed. Loló was always in the thick of things, as she phoned people who'd forgotten about a meeting, suggested ideas for raising money, remembered the dates of festas to be celebrated and activities to be organised, gave Galician lessons three times a week, and on the other days took her laptop and put it on the wine-stained table to give lessons in computing to children who came after school. Lectures had even been put on there, when the secondary school or the council delayed permission to use their premises or simply withheld it with the excuse that A Virandela was getting too involved in politics.

Vicente drank a glass of wine and chatted with Chucho while he waited for the others to emerge from their class. He and his friends were at a low ebb of interest in Trasdás. After the surprise of their arrival, when they were the most discussed piece of news, and then all the finding out and the telling and the asking and the answering, the tide had receded and they were less and less at the centre of conversations as they were absorbed into the life of the town. There were still some loose ends: the boat that had sunk and never been reported; why Rufino's son had come to Trasdás after so many years, penniless. People avoided these unanswered questions and only discussed them behind his back. Chatting, making small talk, was quite sufficient.

'Loló has a proposal for you and your friends,' Chucho said from behind the counter, as he had a glass of wine with Vicente.

'What is it?'

'Wait for the class to end, and then things can be discussed over a bottle of Condado. Loló's unique: if you could get half a dozen like her together they'd make this world go like clockwork,' he said, leaning on the counter over outspread arms as he waited for Vicente to indicate his agreement.

'Well, we'll have to see what it's all about,' Vicente replied without much enthusiasm.

He sat at the table and leafed through the local newspaper. He did so for the sake of doing something, but his head was full of what Chucho had just said. Loló was a busybody, Vicente thought; she'd been a busybody as a child and she'd grown up to be the queen of all busybodies, that's what she was. A right bossy-boots, if they let her she'd take charge of the whole world, and now she wanted to get them involved in A Virandela, for sure. He stood up to go for a glass of wine, and heard the classroom door opening. Shouts and laughs of children and adults surged into the bar. Some pupils left after saying hullo to Chucho, others stayed by the counter for a quick one and after hurried gulps rubbed their hands together, said 'Better go and see if there's any supper for me' and disappeared after buttoning up their raincoats or overcoats by the door.

Andy and Patrick seemed to be the last to come out. Finally they emerged, speaking English into which they introduced the occasional Galician swear-word like '*carallo*' to show that they were making some progress. They approached Vicente, smiling. While Patrick patted him on the back, Andy signalled to Chucho a request for wine. Loló appeared, loaded with books and a radio cassette player that she handed to Chucho to be kept behind the bar.

'We've been listening to some tambourine-players,' said Andy. 'That's real tribal rhythm,' he continued, and added '*meu home*' at the end. Both Andy and Patrick had acquired the habit, when talking to Vicente, of inserting Galician interjections into their English to show him the gigantic steps they were taking in their cultural adaptation.

'Don't call me "*meu home*" – I'm not your man,' said Vicente, shaking his head and adding a '*carallo!*'

'Come on, let's see a bit of good humour on your face – we're just beginners, me and Andy,' Patrick replied.

'What's up, Vicentiño? Why such a long face?' Loló asked as she put her books on the table. 'Your pals here are turning into fine linguists.'

Chucho put a bottle of Condado wine on the table and glasses for everyone, and Loló began to speak, careful to do so slowly: even though Andy and Patrick wouldn't understand much of what she said, she thought it courteous to do this, given the great efforts they were making to follow conversations. In this measured way she explained that she'd worked on her contacts, and A Virandela could organise a winter tour along the coast, even performances in Santiago and A Coruña.

Loló poured the wine and awaited the reply. Andy and Patrick seemed not to understand the details of her proposal, and Vicente remained silent as he sat with legs crossed and smoked.

'What's in it for you people?' he asked, puffing smoke.

'There'd be something for A Virandela – I don't know, twenty per cent or so, we can talk about that. We'd help with publicity and anything else necessary. We need money. The council keeps cutting its funding, and we must have cash to continue our activities.'

Patrick and Andy gazed from side to side, hoping to read in faces what they couldn't understand in words. Patrick asked Vicente to explain what Loló had said. Once Vicente had done so, a broad grin spread over Patrick's face and he nodded happily to Loló.

'We weren't intending to spend winter here,' Vicente eventually said, with scant enthusiasm.

Loló stayed silent as she eyed Vicente and then sipped wine. Patrick and Andy were still gazing at them, trying to guess what they were saying.

'You might have told me that before!' said Loló. 'I must have misunderstood these two: a language problem, no doubt. I thought you wanted work for the winter. If I'd known, I'd have avoided spending money on phone calls – and avoided lots of headaches, too.'

'We do want work to tide us over, but performances for the whole winter are quite another matter.' Seeing that Loló was vexed, Vicente added, 'We're grateful to you, but we must discuss it.'

Andy, tired of gazing at them, managed to stammer in Galician:

'What's up?'

Vicente explained his reply to Patrick and Andy, who made no attempt to conceal their anger. Loló, seeing that they were beginning to argue among themselves and raise their voices, walked to the counter, ordered a dish of octopus, and stayed there chatting to Chucho.

'We came for some fresh air while the Stockwell incident blows over – we didn't plan to stay all winter,' said Vicente.

'Ideas change, that's what they're for. Why are you so keen to go back to London? Why such a hurry to leave?' Patrick retorted, and he stressed the words with taps on the table.

After a while, Loló came back with a dish of octopus and another of squid, and the men moved the glasses and the bottle aside to make room for them. She also brought a basket of bread and some toothpicks, and they all tucked in. After a while, Vicente asked:

'Since when have you two been eating things with suckers?'

9

The pub doors were wide open as the bartenders cleared and cleaned the premises. The group of jugglers had put their props away and were chatting at the bar with the landlord. Their van was parked outside, with their material loaded into it. The long hours of work mingled on the landlord's face with the pride of having witnessed that night in his pub the performance of the clowns that everyone was talking about all along the coast; and on top of that, although he'd brought them there for the publicity, in the end he'd made good money, too.

'Have another before you go,' he said, opening cans of beer.

'I don't want any more – I'm driving back to Trasdás and working tomorrow,' Loló replied, putting her handbag on the bar and waiting for the others to make up their minds.

Patrick and Andy found it hard to communicate with Loló, Nelo and the landlord. But the beers, the laughs and the slaps on the back lubricated language. Loló had offered to help with her van and drive them about, but she'd warned them that now they were doing well they'd have to begin to sort things out for themselves. She'd given them a good start, but it was time for them to stand on their own feet. Because of the group, she was neglecting A Virandela, and whenever she drove them to their shows she went to work the next day with bags under her eyes.

'Those two are overstepping the mark, someone had better go and fetch them,' said Loló, and showed the others her watch. 'It's half past midnight: say half an hour to Trasdás, then the unloading, and it'll be half past one before I see my bed.'

The others exchanged glances and picked up their glasses of beer, each hoping that someone else might volunteer to go for Vicente and Milagros. They all realised it was one of those delicate situations in which it was better to wait and see. Vicente and Milagros had gone for a stroll on the quayside when the show ended, and still hadn't returned.

'Yes, to be honest we must close, too,' said the landlord, with embraces over the counter to Patrick and Andy. 'I've already told you, my friends,' (this last word in English), 'that you're welcome here, and now I say so again.'

They put their caps on and went out into the cold of the night. In front of the pub Milagros's car was also parked. In it was a friend who'd come with her to the show. When she saw them leaving the pub, she approached them, rubbing her arms to keep them warm.

'They seem to be taking rather long,' the young woman remarked.

'Someone will have to go and tell them it's time to leave,' said Loló.

'I'll go,' said the young woman, hunched up in the cold, 'but perhaps someone could come with me.'

'Hey, you, Nelo,' said Loló, 'go with her to fetch them, we must be moving.'

'Look, there they are,' said Nelo, relieved.

Emerging from among the nets and strolling towards the middle of the quay came Vicente and Milagros, unaware that the others were waiting for them. They seemed cheerful as they lit cigarettes. As they approached, Milagros glanced at her watch and they hastened their pace.

'Have you been waiting long?' asked Vicente, surprised.

'Just a bit. Come on,' Loló retorted on her way to the van.

Nelo was pointing the coastal towns out to Patrick, who, when he recognised a place where they'd performed, declared with pride:

'We've been there.'

Loló called the others and they entered the van while Milagros got into her car with her friend, signalling to Vicente to phone her. He sat in the back of the van with Andy and the props. They drove on to the main road without exchanging many words, and Vicente rolled another cigarette. When they'd been on the road for some time, Patrick commented:

'This time you didn't need custard tarts,' and he burst out laughing. Andy laughed, too.

Vicente made no reply as he gazed through the window at the damp night, the villages along the coast, the sea and the small boats heading for harbour.

'Don't you miss it?' he asked Nelo, who was sitting in the front with Loló and Patrick.

'Miss what?' Nelo replied, looking back.

Vicente gestured towards the sea as he lit his cigarette. Nelo looked ahead again, and after a while he said:

'The sea?'

No reply came from Vicente. Nelo added:

'No.'

'It was a job of work,' said Loló. 'What'll you do now? Clear stuff up for this lot?'

'I was tired of going to sea. I got a good pay-off.'

'And when it's spent,' said Loló, eyeing him, 'when it's spent, what then? Your parents were really upset. These aren't times to be quitting a job.'

'Something better will turn up.'

Loló didn't reply, and drove on in silence. After a while she asked:

'What's all this about custard tarts?'

Patrick pointed at himself to enquire whether the question was meant for him.

'Yes, I heard you talk about custard tarts. What's all this about custard tarts?'

Patrick drew some tarts on the misty windscreen. Then, as he pointed at Vicente and sniggered, he stammered in Galician:

'It's what he feeds women with.'

'What he feeds women with?'

In the back of the van, where Andy was beginning to nod off, Vicente laughed. That night had been without doubt the best since their arrival. Milagros had dissipated the strange sensations that had enervated him and distanced him from his surroundings. The sheen on her face, her silky skin and that smile, always ready to play on her mouth. Milagros had made him feel, for the first time since they'd come here, the sense of the word 'home'. The place to which one returns: that was what she meant for him, it was as if she'd meant it for years. Perhaps so, or perhaps it was the beer he'd drunk during and after the performance. He had a perfect recollection of her face and its expressions, which, like the glow-worms and the zigzagging leaps over puddles, seemed to have been waiting to appear unexpectedly.

'Vicente, what's all this about custard tarts?' asked Loló.

'Your fast-learning pupils can explain it,' said Vicente as he continued to daydream and gaze out of the window.

Patrick repeated, laughing fit to burst:

'When he fancies a woman he feeds her custard tarts that the Portuguese make in London,' and he clapped a hand to his mouth to try to cover his laughter.

Loló and Nelo smiled in surprise. Andy was struggling to stay awake, rubbing his eyes and his arms.

Vicente continued gazing at the sea through the misty windows with a half-smile on his lips, waiting for them to change the subject; but Patrick didn't seem willing to let it die. He glanced back and asked Andy to confirm his account:

'Am I right or not, Andy?'

Andy, curled up in a corner, replied:

'I don't know. When he takes girls out he does give them custard tarts.'

They all burst out laughing again, and Andy went on:

'It's the ritual of carnal love.'

The general laughter continued. Vicente was leaning against the side of the van with his legs stretched out, smiling to himself every so often. A little later, when the hilarity was subsiding, Loló commented:

'My little English lad, what a lot you've learnt in those English lands – giving custard tarts to unfortunate women!'

'I learnt juggling, too,' said Vicente.

'Well, take care not to throw too much into the air at the same time.'

The van took the curve at A Muiñeira, and the bridge over the ria swung into view. Vicente raised his head to contemplate the bridge again. Before long they entered Trasdás, drove to the house and unloaded the material they used in their performances. Loló said goodbye and the others stood in the doorway and decided what to do.

'We can go to the fishermen's bar for a brandy,' said Patrick. 'A nice glass of brandy wouldn't be a bad idea, to help the digestion along.'

They started to walk downhill, Nelo silent in their midst, by now used to their speaking English to each other. He'd left his fishing job a few days earlier, and ever since then he'd stayed with the group all the time.

'We could go to the Forum,' said Nelo, breaking the silence, before they reached the main road. 'We can listen to music there.'

'But it's quite far away, better the fishermen's bar,' said Patrick. 'It's just over there.'

The three made to cross the road to go to the fishermen's bar on the quay, and saw Nelo standing still under the light of a street lamp at the roadside, looking down at the ground.

'I'd better go home. I'm really tired,' he said, hands in pockets. 'See you tomorrow.'

The others watched Nelo climb the steps up to the old part of Trasdás. Then they exchanged glances, lit cigarettes and walked down to the quay, which was fading into the night mist. In the background they could see the lights of lorries and open bars, and people wheeling boxes of fish this way and that.

10

Maybe his housemates were right, and spending the winter in Trasdás wasn't such a bad idea – if it weren't for the bridge, and those hurtful looks aimed at the back of his head, and his uncle, and Loló's sarcasm when she called him her little English lad.

After the day of the performance in the pub in Argalo, Vicente had phoned Milagros and they'd agreed to meet in Porto Trapeiro, in a cafeteria there. She'd made smiles appear more than usual on his face, and had allowed Andy and Patrick to nurture hopes that he might calm down, for the winter at least.

Vicente awoke with cold sweats on the day of the date. He shaved, then passed the time in a hot bath with his eyes shut, trying to unravel dreams or nightmares.

But he kept reaching a point at which the cold crept up his back and the bridge over the ria displayed its most metallic colours. All his good humour of the previous days had disappeared without warning, without explanation, and now here he was in a hot bath surrounded by foam, attempting to understand an unease for which he could find no explanation.

The others had gone away that morning, and there was nothing for him to do except wait for the time to come for the date with Milagros. Andy and Patrick returned for lunch and sat in the kitchen discussing what they had to do that afternoon and how things were going. Conversations about the Lizard, London, and how to return there had, as time passed, become less frequent. It was almost always Vicente who had to broach these subjects: London seemed, for Andy and Patrick, to belong to a distant past that was no longer theirs. When they left, Vicente was tempted to call Milagros to cancel their date that evening. There was still time. He could give her any excuse, for example that he didn't feel well.

From the window he saw cars being parked along the main road, and people stopping to go into the bars and shops. Fishermen walking with bags of sandwiches and fruit to the boats, and children with school bags on their backs. He had a sensation of immobility. He felt static, his feet weighted with ballast, his limbs stiff and numb.

It exasperated him that he couldn't understand the swings of mood that were taking charge of him and holding him back. He was going to see Milagros, who'd been able to remove from his face the glumness that had marked it ever since his arrival in Trasdás. She'd made him laugh. She'd contrived to rip open a net in which he'd been caught. He could still feel the relaxation in his cheek muscles after that laugh. It had come unexpectedly, like a gust of wind on his eyes that had turned into an inner breeze and changed his mood. But now, just a few hours from meeting her again, here he was running his fingers along the damp edges of the window-panes and directing a wishful gaze towards the space under the bridge, a space for flight. Milagros, he longed to see her; Milagros, he feared seeing her.

She'd seen the bridge being built and she'd seen people come and go. She'd lived in the knowledge that men board boats and flee with the excuse of seeking fish along that line always at the end of the ria, and she'd heard the sound of engines fading into the distance. She'd stayed here and knew about all that. Whichever decision he took, to remain in Trasdás or return to London, she'd be here to see him do one thing or the other. She held the secret of time, while he still didn't understand the secret of space.

The hours went by and he couldn't pluck up the courage to cancel the date, nor could he wipe that damp, uncontrollable longing from his face. Sometimes he wanted to slap it and hide beneath its skin the look that kept appearing in such an unexpected and inexorable way.

He searched in vain for something to wear instead of that loose, grubby raincoat, but in the end he put it on before the mirror. He set out towards the main road to wait for the bus to Porto Trapeiro. The rain was making people hurry, and those waiting were huddled and squeezed together at the bus stop. There were many children with folders who came to Trasdás to study with private tutors and were returning home. Vicente joined the group, shivering, his hands in his raincoat pockets.

When they boarded the bus, the driver spoke briefly to each new passenger, especially the girls, who replied with a shake of their heads; and even when they were seated he talked on, in shouts. Nobody said anything to Vicente, but he heard a few words in hushed tones among groups where he'd been recognised as one of the clowns, and where they pointed at him behind his back.

He left the bus and walked towards the harbour. He went by the fish market and got in the way of busy fishwives, dealers and fishermen. He entered a steakhouse where lorry drivers were drinking glasses of brandy and cups of coffee. They were talking in loud voices, and the whole place seemed to be part of one enormous incessant din. He looked at the shelves, the football pennants and the calendars, and examined the workers' sunburnt faces. People with fond feelings for a lorry, the sea, a job of work, fish, with caps pulled down to their ears; he listened to their words, brimming with sense, direct, and when they complained that there were no fish left in the sea they stared into the distance and he saw emptiness in their eye sockets. He was getting drunk on so much looking, and he'd almost forgotten what he'd come to Porto Trapeiro to do. Before the barman could serve him, he left and strode off towards the Nordés.

As he came closer to this cafeteria, where he'd agreed to meet Milagros, he slowed down to prepare his mind for the meeting, for the date, and to gather strength for the effort he was going to have to make. He entered Lizard Square through the Middle Gate and saw Milagros lock her car door and go into the Nordés. He remained in the dark square.

Milagros sat at a table near the bar and opened a newspaper. Vicente watched her from the arcade as he lit a cigarette. It'd be great to sit with her and chat about old times, about their lives. He stayed where he was, smoking his cigarette and watching the drizzle fall through the light of the street lamps. A little later she got to her feet and went to the toilet, and when she returned he thought she'd spotted him in the street, so he made as if to walk towards the cafeteria; but she sat down without any signs of having seen him. The waiter approached her table and served her a soft drink, and she lifted the newspaper to make room for the glass and the nibbles.

She finished reading the newspaper, folded it, and placed it on the table. She glanced at her watch and lit a cigarette, with an eye on the television. Vicente recalled the happy conversation they'd enjoyed the other day on the quay while the others waited for them. They'd kept giggling nervously, like two uneasy, jittery adolescents exploring the opposite sex. It had been so agreeable to watch the boats coming and going as they sheltered by the ice factory and smoked, their fingers numb from the cold!

Images passed before Vicente's eyes as in an old film, agreeable images that filled him with a certain pleasure, desired images. A beach in the summer, he with

Milagritos and Carmela, a barbecue with sardines over it in the Ventoso pine-grove; Carmela was about to play in the sand, and the sunbeams were gilding Milagritos's body. Milagritos, the woman with eyes like the sea. They were images in faded colours as if they belonged to a relived past, and they were accompanied by the scraping sound of the projector, as in an old cinema.

Again she glanced at her watch. Half an hour had elapsed since her arrival. She went to the bar and asked to use the telephone. Vicente contemplated her slender body leaning on the bar; she laughed as she spoke to someone at the other end of the line. When she'd finished, she sat down again for a couple of minutes, then took her purse from her handbag and went to the bar to pay. Calmly, glancing at the television, she put her raincoat on and picked up her handbag. She said goodbye to the bartender and walked to her car. Vicente hid behind a pillar and watched her get in. He heard the engine starting and watched the car's lights disappearing down the street. He emerged from behind the pillar and went back to the bus stop.

The bus carried fewer people on the return journey, and it was quieter. When it reached Trasdás he walked to the house. His mates were out. It was about ten, and they must be with the A Virandela people.

Vicente wandered from one part of the house to another, unable to settle down; finally he rummaged in the kitchen cupboards and poured himself a large brandy. He took a swig, which he retained in his mouth as he used a forefinger to wipe away a drop trickling from his lips. Then he slumped into the rocking-chair that faced the window and gazed out at the band of night contained between two tall buildings, as if he were in the stalls of a theatre at the top of the centre aisle that leads towards the stage. He only interrupted this resolute immobility to bring the glass to his lips and from time to time pour more brandy into it.

Suddenly he rose and, stumbling into the kitchen table and groping his way along the corridor, reached his bedroom. He picked up his Pierrot costume, spread it on his bed, gazed at it and slowly put it on. He took his make-up, whitened his face, and painted a black smile round his mouth.

He examined himself in the bathroom mirror, returned to the kitchen, switched the light off and dropped back into the rocking-chair, glass in hand. Each time he began to nod off he clutched the glass and took a swig as if in search of help to stay awake. He left the glass on the floor and rocked in the chair. His cap dropped from his head and, as he swayed back and forth, he fell asleep.

Keys clinked at the front door and voices approached the kitchen. The light came on and Vicente rubbed his eyes and blinked, but remained in the same state of motionless half-sleep before the window. Andy and Nelo came in and put a tray of small horse mackerel on the table. Nelo opened a can of beer and gave it to Andy, who drank from it and handed it back.

'Where are the others?' Nelo asked.

'They went out – Patrick with Loló, and Vicente with that Milagritos woman.'

Nelo lit a cigarette, inhaled deeply, and offered the

beer to Andy again. He drank, and the two men gazed at each other. Andy moved his hand towards the hand that Nelo had placed on the table and caressed it without taking his gaze away. Nelo turned his hand over and the two sets of fingers intertwined. Then the men melted into a tight embrace and kissed, the hands of each behind the other's head, caressing his locks.

Nelo leant his chin on Andy's shoulder, and they remained for some time with their bodies pressed together. Then Nelo tapped Andy on the back.

'Look,' he murmured into his ear, pointing at Pierrot's fallen cap.

Andy disengaged from Nelo and went over to the rocking-chair. Vicente's eyes were fastened on the dark of the night. Andy glanced through the window and looked again at Vicente, motionless, his black smile smudged and his whitened chin streaked by the drops of brandy that had trickled from his mouth. Andy drew the curtains like someone closing a theatre curtain, but Vicente-Pierrot remained motionless. Nelo walked over and they dragged him to his room.

11

Winter hadn't yet arrived, but there had already been storms that had sunk small boats anchored by the harbour wall. These were signs of what many were already predicting: a winter like those of years back. The water was almost always choppy, and boats rocked on their way to the open sea. Skies were grey, and dense clouds often covered the bridge right down to the water.

The days had drifted by since Vicente's failure to keep his date with Milagros. Making the most of the intervals between cloudbursts, he went for strolls on the beach, along the harbour wall, and to Miñato's bar, from where the coast on the other side of the ria could be glimpsed through the arches of the bridge. He particularly enjoyed walks after rain, when the dampness that had soaked into the sand mingled with the sea breeze, in which the scent of the tossing waves floated. Miñato's wife would bring him a glass of cherry brandy when she saw him come in, and he'd go and sit by the window to spend the grey hours in scrutiny of the movements of the clouds.

At night-time he'd go to the fishermen's bar and listen to them chatting when they came back from the sea. They didn't mind him listening, and perhaps turned their heads in his direction when he wasn't looking and murmured a few words to each other until, with an effort to stay upright, he croaked a 'goodnight' to which nobody replied.

One cool afternoon with brief flurries of rain, Vicente paid for his glasses of cherry brandy, turned his raincoat collar up and went for a stroll along the edge of the beach. He saw René, not far from the harbour wall, as usual. He was heaving on a crate the tide had washed up. He'd lashed a rope to it, thrown the rope over his shoulder and was dragging it from the reach of the waves. Vicente went over and helped him pull it up the beach. Once well away from the sea they stopped and used an old piece of iron to smash a hole in the wood. Through it René extracted a cardboard box that he made haste to open in search of treasure, and found a glass sphere with a Father Christmas inside. He turned it upside-down, turned it the right way up again, and tiny snowflakes cascaded down.

'You can make some money when Christmas comes if you take them to Señor Valentín in the big hardware store,' said Vicente.

'I must keep a look-out, maybe some more will turn up,' said René.

Vicente walked on towards town beside René as he dragged the crate home and called to his grandmother; she emerged, drying her hands on her apron, and Vicente stopped for a moment to watch the boy take the glass sphere out, turn it and hold it up for her to see. She clapped her hands and laughed, then she peered into the crate and clapped again. She caught sight of Vicente waiting there and said:

'Have you seen this?' and then with a laugh in René's direction, 'You little scamp, there's nothing the sea spits out you don't grab hold of!'

Vicente headed for home, alien to the streets he climbed and the people he met. Trasdás seemed a town inhabited by spirits without human form. A doll's house with toy figures waiting for a child to pick them up and shift them from place to place. A stage with puppets hanging from strings worked by the wind. He felt trapped on that stage, like an abandoned puppet whose strings nobody pulled, an actor without a dialogue and without a mask.

When evening came, he went to Chucho's bar: the A Virandela lesson would soon be over, and it had been some time since he'd last gone there to wait for his friends. He hadn't phoned Milagros, not even to apologise: he didn't know what to say. He could simply claim he'd been unwell, but several days had gone by and, even if he hadn't been able to phone her because he was ill in bed, he could have sent a message. The warmth of the cherry brandy was rising from his stomach. He didn't want to lie to her, but he didn't want to tell her the truth, either.

Night was falling fast, and even the street lamps seemed to emit less light as autumn slunk away and winter crept up like a voracious wolf nosing out the prey it's about to attack. Dogs became more nocturnal behind cars, and passers-by more solitary, not raising their heads, to avoid the risk of having to say hello to someone. Vicente crossed the road so as not to walk by the cafeteria owned by his uncle, who was behind the counter chatting to customers, and continued along the main road to Chucho's bar.

Andy and Patrick were seated at a table with Loló and Roberto, another of the active members of A Virandela. Vicente caught Chucho's eye and asked for a glass of Condado. Vicente stayed silent while the others continued a wine-warmed discussion. They were laughing and explaining words in Galician and English to each other. Nobody seemed keen to interrupt the flow of speech and bring Vicente into the conversation. There was a moment of silence, when all looks converged on him. Roberto gestured to Chucho, who opened a bottle of Condado, carried it to their table and took the opportunity to collect empty plates.

'What's up, my little English lad?... Seems you don't remember what winters are like over here.'

'I remember perfectly,' Vicente retorted, and put the glass of Condado to his lips. He then repeated, 'I remember perfectly.'

'Nowadays, with the changing climate, they aren't always like that. You never know what's coming.'

‘Whatever sort of winter it is, I won’t spend it here,’ Vicente declared.

All gazes converged on him as he looked down to take tobacco from his pocket and roll a cigarette. The others watched his dexterous movements and waited for him to explain what he’d just said.

Impatiently Patrick demanded:

‘What did you say?’

‘Winter won’t catch me here,’ said Vicente as he took his first drag. After a pause he continued, ‘In a few days I’m off to London. When I know how things stand there, I’ll phone and we’ll decide what to do.’

‘What about Saturday’s performance?’ Patrick interrupted, in English.

‘It’ll have to be cancelled,’ said Vicente.

Loló rose to her feet and picked up her raincoat without a word; Roberto waved goodbye to Andy and Patrick and went with her to pay at the bar. Andy and Patrick were staring at Vicente in astonishment. Patrick went up to Loló to tell her to calm down and wait for him, but she replied with a shake of her head as she left.

‘When did you come up with that decision?’ Patrick asked, with a frown.

‘Today. It makes no sense for us to stay stuck in this hole,’ said Vicente, nibbling a fingernail and looking away.

Andy leant back in his chair snorting, poured himself more wine and signalled with his finger for Vicente to give him tobacco and cigarette papers.

‘How can we cancel the performance?’ asked Patrick.

Vicente stayed silent, his gaze fixed on the door, and Andy sat stiff with crossed arms and the cigarette smoking in his hand. Patrick put an elbow on the table and rested his bowed head on his hand. He turned to Andy and shot out:

'Haven't you got anything to say?'

Andy, unperturbed, flicked ash into the ashtray, shrugged and resumed his stiff stance.

'Haven't you got anything to say?' Patrick insisted, in amazement.

'No, I haven't much to say,' said Andy calmly.

'So this bugger decides just like that to clear off and leave us in the lurch with the performances we're committed to, and you haven't got anything to say?' Patrick repeated in fury.

'I'd like him to stay, but I could see it coming.'

'You could see it coming?' retorted Patrick. 'Something's going on here that I don't know about. Can you explain, Vicente, why you have to clear off all of a sudden?'

'It isn't all of a sudden.'

'It isn't all of a sudden?' Patrick exclaimed, planting both elbows on the table and his chin on his hands.

They remained thus, in silence, with a lamp shining on to the tops of their heads. The three bodies were motionless, isolated, speechless. Chucho, his arms crossed over the counter, eyed the men left at the table. Patrick raised his black, snub-nosed face every so often to glance from Andy to Vicente, awaiting an explanation. Vicente was seated at an angle and Andy looked at his tense profile, tight lips struggling to contain the words that could explain his decision. Chucho continued watching the movements of the men at the table. They were like actors who longed for words but had forgotten their dialogue, before a single spectator.

'Anyone for any more?'

12

Vicente went motionless up the escalator at Brixton station. On the escalator opposite, severe, inscrutable faces of black men in baseball caps, colourful jackets and loose trousers went down, together with people of other races and appearances. They were like two automated queues, one leaving a stage and the other entering it. The ticket barriers were what separated the wings from the stage, and the men with long dishevelled hair and burning eyes who asked people for their day passes to sell them on were the first signs that the performance was about to start.

As soon as Vicente left the station and saw small puddles and a wet street, he regretted not having brought the raincoat that had done him such good service in

Trasdás. He turned left towards the street market. The stalls were being cleared away, and he didn't want to miss this, the best time to haggle, even though he didn't yet know where he was going to sleep. He bought bananas, apples and a packet of cakes, and put it all in the bag with changes of clothes he'd brought with him.

He headed for a squat that hippies had taken over in one of the streets parallel to the market. He hoped it was still there, because the squatters had received frequent threats of eviction. He didn't like to mix with that lot – new travellers, crusties with dogs, hippies – but they were the only ones who were organised and knew about the empty squats in the area. He knocked on the door and a lanky character with a tattooed neck looked him up and down and let him in; he told him not to make any noise, because a meditation session was in progress in the basement, and gestured towards the stairway, festooned with graffiti.

This building had once been a factory, of which only the skeleton of walls and partitions remained. In the lower part they held parties and carried out other activities, and in the upper part there was a vegetarian café run by different people each night. In it they put on shows, poetry readings and exhibitions, screened home-made films and organised jam sessions that lasted into the early morning. Vicente knew the place and the sort of people there. He'd dropped in with the others from time to time: you could take your own drink, and the food was very cheap.

He climbed the stairs slowly, paying attention to the notices on the walls in case there were any that indicated where he could sleep that night. The lanky man loped past him up to the first floor. When Vicente drew the curtain at the top, he saw two Rastas with two blondes in dreadlocks, smoking joints and guffawing. Two other couples were talking at a table that had a notebook on it, and there was a girl reading a book. The tables, all different, acquired from skips and junk shops or donated, had coloured plastic sheets and half-used candles in bottles on top of them.

At the counter Vicente ordered a cup of tea from the tattooed lanky man, who'd returned to his post, and left his bag on a table. When the tea was ready he went to get it, and asked the man if he knew of any empty squats. The man asked the girl who was with him in the kitchen. As she continued cooking she replied that he'd have to speak to Robert – he was the one who handled such matters. The lanky man turned back with an obliging smile:

'We only come here once a week – you must speak to Robert, that guy over there,' and he pointed towards a man with long hair tied into two buns, one of the group seated round the notebook. 'The trouble is he's in a meeting right now – better wait a bit.'

Vicente sat down and rolled a cigarette. From time to time he glanced at the table where this Robert character was sitting, and where suddenly raised voices alternated with laughter. Robert was the one who was becoming most heated as they talked, while the others tried to reason with references to numbers, sums of money and dates.

They took a break and, while one of the group walked over to the counter, the man called Robert went to the toilet. When he returned, he sat down with the appearance of one who was dead beat and could feel smoke coming out of his ears. Vicente took the chance to go and ask him if he knew of any empty squats in the area.

'I'm in a meeting. I've got quite enough on my plate. You'll have to wait.'

'I don't mind, I can wait over there,' Vicente replied, indicating a sofa by the window.

Robert continued facing the others with his back turned to Vicente, who went to sit on the sofa and began to roll a cigarette. He looked all round the room: there were posters about parties and demonstrations, graffiti, and coloured curtains, all hanging in total disorder. He fidgeted on the sofa, shifted his legs about and put his feet up on a chair. Robert's chatter continued and Vicente started to lose patience: the dude was making him wait just to display his power.

'If you don't tell me where there are empty squats, when you draw that curtain tomorrow what you're first going to see are my pants and socks hanging in the middle of this café,' Vicente declared.

The Rasta group stopped laughing and those at Robert's table exchanged glances, unable to make much sense of his attitude. He turned and looked sidelong at Vicente.

'In an hour's time a film show starts – can you give me any reason why I need bother with you?'

'You're as keen to see me out of here as I am to go,' Vicente answered, puffing smoke towards the ceiling.

Robert thought for a moment.

'That's a good reason,' he replied, and got up and went behind the curtain. A door creaked, he returned with some stapled-together papers and approached Vicente.

'Here you are. None of what's written here is necessarily correct – it's all put together with the information that reaches us, and everything can change without us knowing,' Robert observed, returning to his table.

The first page was a map of Brixton, Stockwell, Clapham, part of Streatham, Camberwell and Kennington. Squares represented empty buildings and red dots squats where there were people but room for more. Crosses were squats from which the squatters had been evicted.

On the other pages were the squats' addresses together with notes about matters such as whether electricity and gas were connected. Vicente was surprised to find that the squat where they'd lived was marked with a square, indicating it was empty.

He considered where the buildings were located and then examined the other pages to see if there was any information about their condition. He only wanted a temporary place, he didn't know how long for – a week, a fortnight, enough to find out how things stood; and then when the others came back they could all look for something more permanent.

He put the papers down on the table and tried to think about what he hadn't considered during the days previous to his journey, not even during the journey itself. What had he come to London to do? There were loose ends that tangled with others. What had become of the Lizard? Did he know anything about the results of the investigation into the killing in the off-licence? In other words, were they free of suspicion? Better not even think about Reddy – or perhaps he should think about him? Vicente had never understood that night's events, the lover's attitude: why didn't she tell him straightaway that she'd found Vicente in the sitting-room rummaging in the gilt cash tin? If she didn't tell him at the time, what would have been the sense of telling him later? And what about Jane? No doubt she didn't even remember him, he'd left without saying goodbye, without saying anything, and now he'd seem like a ghost if he turned up.

Where did he want to stay? What did he want to be near? Something was calling him to Stockwell, but he didn't want to stay in the house where he'd lived with his friends, not even close to it. It might be under surveillance, the police would have warned the neighbours. Someone might recognise him.

There was a big house on the boundary between Stockwell and Clapham. It had Stockwell's insularity and was near the Common, the pubs and the shops. Electricity and gas were connected and no-one was living there, if the information in those papers was correct. Vicente also made a note of the address of a house high on Brixton Hill, near Streatham, just in case.

Then he went away, leaving the papers on Robert's table. Robert called out:

'My pleasure.'

'Mine too.'

Vicente walked to the centre of Brixton, and near the Town Hall he caught a bus. It was the route he'd travelled so many times, except that now he went on to Clapham. Night was falling, and it occurred to him that a torch wouldn't be a bad idea. He spotted a second-hand ironmonger's and got off the bus. He yelled to the old man who was closing the shop door, went in and asked for a torch. The man, wearing a raincoat as an overall, brought him a box of torches, and Vicente chose one with a round glass cover. It sent out a semicircle of rather feeble light. He dropped a pound into the hand of the old man, who grumbled with him to the door.

Now, as it began to grow dark on this drizzly day, was when Clapham's many pubs and restaurants were most evident, with their illuminated signs and their windows packed with moneyed young people who like to be in the atmosphere of South London but for whom Brixton is too South London.

Vicente walked with his bag to the Common, turned left, then left again – and there was Truro Road. He sauntered along it. There were several houses that showed few signs of life – curtains drawn, no lights – but the one he'd made a note of really did seem uninhabited. He approached it, the front door was locked, he forced the gate into the back garden and went through. The small windows by the passage into the garden were in a bad state, and the glass was broken on the door into a small conservatory that led to the kitchen. It was easy to force the door open, and in he went.

He lit his torch. The floor was damp, strewn with rubbish. He walked on, peering into rooms: there were graffiti on the walls, the wallpaper had been torn down in strips. The wooden floors squeaked, and if there was anyone in the house they knew by now that someone else was there. He climbed the stairs; the banisters wobbled and some of the wooden uprights were missing. At the top of the stairs his inspection continued.

Nobody seemed to have lived there for some time, not even squatters: he saw a few old discarded syringes, but the house didn't seem to have been recently used. He continued opening doors and peering into rooms. He'd already seen a couple, one downstairs and the other on the first floor, that still had their fitted carpets and where he could sleep. He reached the last room, pushed the door open, glimpsed a flurry of movement and felt something cold slicing across his hand at speed.

'Shit,' and he jumped back as the door slammed shut.

'Leave us alone,' someone behind it said in a choking voice.

Vicente dropped his bag and, torch in hand, gave the door a shove with his foot; he heard a body falling, and the door remained ajar. He gave it two more shoves and managed to open it. He shone his torch in and saw two puny, scrawny figures, one behind the other, agitated and fearful. Warily he swung the torch from side to side, trying to make the room out, and in its faint light he could divine rather than see two pairs of children's eyes, gleaming and weary. The protective figure was a boy with a knife in one hand, shouting nervously in a hoarse voice as if struggling for breath. His other hand was over his eyes to shield them from the glare of the torch; behind him a girl's terrified face poked out every so often.

'Leave us alone. Scram or I'll kill you,' the boy screamed.

'Look what you've done,' said Vicente, and showed him his hand. A dribble of blood ran down from the back of it between his fingers.

'I'll do more than that if you don't leave us alone,' the boy retorted in a tiresome, feeble voice, like a trickle of air struggling out of his throat.

In the room there were piles of bottles, some with candle-ends in them, and cartons containing blankets. A chemical smell assailed Vicente's nostrils.

'Put that knife away, right now – do you see me carrying a weapon?' he said in a reassuring tone to calm the children down.

The girl bent over, grabbed a bottle and again took up her position behind the boy, who was brandishing the knife in his outstretched hand.

'I haven't come to do you any harm. I'm just looking for a place to sleep. How was I to know that someone lived here?'

'You know now,' the boy replied, plucking up courage and approaching the door to shut it.

Vicente took the chance to seize his hand and wrest the knife from him. The boy jumped back and the girl gave him her bottle and went for another one.

'You bloody children. I have the knife now – can't you see I don't want to harm you? Now listen carefully: I'm going to a room downstairs and I don't want anyone to come and bother me. Is that clear?'

Vicente wrapped a handkerchief round his hand. It was a shallow wound, but bad enough to stain his shirtsleeves and stamp his arrival in London and his installation in the squat with a bad beginning. He descended the stairs more noisily than he'd climbed them, so that the youngsters could tell he was no longer on the first floor, and entered the carpeted room.

He put his bag down and went to inspect the meters. They were indeed connected, but the youngsters, not realising this, hadn't switched the heating on. He did so and returned to the room he'd chosen to sleep in.

He didn't have any bedclothes for that night, but he wasn't sure he wanted to stay there. Those kids could only bring trouble. They were weak, vulnerable, shitting themselves with fear and, what was more, they must be spending their days sniffing glue and other such stuff. They were a fucking problem. The boy had a Scottish accent, they must have run away and be living on the streets. Vicente paced several times round the room and cursed his luck. It'd be better to try the other house he'd jotted down. His hand had stopped bleeding. He heard the door upstairs creak, and then footsteps and shouts:

'Hey you – still there?'

'Yes,' Vicente replied, going out into the corridor.

'What do you want here?' The boy spoke with his head over the banisters, and the girl's head could be divined behind it like a shadow.

'I want to sleep, that's all – what else could I want?'

'We've no problem with that. You can stay.'

'Is anyone looking for you?'

'No.'

Vicente was pacing from the corridor to the front door and back into the corridor. He entered his room, picked up his bag, went back out and yelled:

'To tell you the truth, I think I'm the one who doesn't want me to stay here – I don't want to stay with people who greet me with a jackknife.'

'We didn't know who it might be,' the boy shouted in the same sickly voice, 'but now we know you're OK, you can stay.'

'No thank you very much, I think I'll go and look for somewhere else,' said Vicente, shutting the door of his room.

'Do stay, please.'

This was also a wretched, diseased voice, but it communicated a certain gentleness. For the first time the girl had uttered a few words. Her voice had pierced him like a wire along his spine, it was a hurtful, querulous, tender, ailing voice. Vicente, torch in one hand and bag in the other, looked up and saw the girl's face beside the boy's. He held his bag out.

'I've got some cakes and fruit. You can come down.'

The youngsters began to creep down the stairs, keeping their heads over the banisters, holding hands and getting in each other's way. When they were near the bottom they stopped and stared at Vicente from their fearful height.

He opened his bag and held cakes and fruit out to them. The girl had her thumb in her mouth, and her head was rocking in uncontrollable movement. The boy accepted the invitation and began to eat.

'I've switched the heating on,' Vicente said.

In the end the girl took a piece of banana, bit it listlessly and coughed with the chesty cough of a grown man. In that semi-darkness it was hard to process shadows and glimmers of light and make out two thin, undernourished faces. It didn't seem a recent deprivation, rather an inherited, congenital hunger, a hunger of neglected, unloved children. They had bulging eyes with a red glow in them.

'Have you come from far away?'

The youngsters didn't reply, they hardly lifted their heads.

'Are you on drugs?'

'No,' the boy replied, interrupting his concentration on the food, while the girl, seated now, continued her head movements, her thumb still in her mouth.

'Aren't you eating any more than that?' Vicente asked her.

'I'm not hungry.'

Vicente, leaning on the banisters, watched the boy eat. He checked his wound, and then decided to try a piece of carrot cake.

'I see you two don't much feel like talking.'

'How long are you going to stay?' the girl asked, removing her thumb from her mouth. The way she spoke left Vicente confused, the questions of a child in the voice of an old woman.

'I don't know. I'll stay today, or a few days at least.' It didn't seem a good idea to remain there with those kids, and he didn't know why he'd replied that he would, for a few days. But now he'd said it he didn't want to change his mind straightaway. They didn't reply, the girl had stopped her head-rocking and replaced it with a new movement of her legs, which she opened and closed. The boy sat in a somewhat soporiferous state, his belly full after the great banquet.

'I'm Vicente. And you are...?'

'I'm Laurie, and this is Danny.'

'Well, Laurie and Danny, I'm going out now. When I come back, would you like me to warn you somehow that it is me, so you don't need to reach for your knife?' As he said this, he realised that he was the one who had the knife now, and for a moment he was undecided whether to give it back or keep it. All three became aware at the same time of this moment of indecision.

'You can bang three times on your door,' said Danny.

'All right, that's what I'll do.' He delved into his pockets and offered the knife to the boy, who seemed to awake from his half-sleep and calmly took it.

The youngsters went upstairs and Vicente entered his room, put his bag on the floor and went round piling rubbish up in a corner. A little later there was a knock on the door.

'Who is it?'

The door opened and Danny came in with a sleeping-bag.

'We don't need this, we've lots of blankets up there.'

'Cheers,' said Vicente, taking the sleeping-bag as he winked at the boy.

The two looked at each other without a word, then Danny raised a thumb and left. Vicente felt an urge to go for a stroll. Ever since his arrival, an idea had been hovering round his head, coming and going; it was like an attack of scabies, an itch it was hard to overlook. He wanted to return to the scene of the crime, even if only to pass by on the other side of the street and peer into the off-licence from there.

He left the squat and strolled towards Clapham. It was about ten at night, and people were leaving restaurants and walking to pubs or getting into taxis waiting with open doors. Cars raced past on wet tyres with that sibilant sound that mothers make to help their children to wee. A group of men in football scarves and shirts were arguing at a pub door, and people waiting for buses were sending sidelong glances towards them, fearful that a brawl might break out at any moment.

He walked on as far as Clapham Common and there he turned towards Stockwell. The streets were becoming less busy and the passers-by quieter as they hurried to reach their destinations and leave that void of shopless streets behind them. His hands were in his jacket pockets and he was looking down at the ground.

After walking for ten minutes in the cold drizzle he reached the street of the off-licence they'd robbed. He could see its lights, it was on his side of the street. He walked on with his head bowed and tried to behave in a completely normal way and ignore his heartbeats, which seemed to be galloping on top of each other. He didn't intend to go in but walk past and see if there had been any changes in the shop – if grilles, warnings or alarms had been installed. He looked up: the shop was on a corner and he was about to pass it. He lingered as if he were about to cross the street and a car were coming, then he edged along and glanced through the shop door.

And in there, through the glass, he saw a bulky man in a turban. He rubbed his eyes to sharpen his vision and, astonished, almost slipping over on the kerb, he thought it could be the shop assistant that he'd shot. He continued to stare, caught in a net of sensations that almost made him shudder: he clearly remembered that the assistant had been a huge Sikh with a big nose. The man was talking and laughing with a customer. Vicente walked on, staggered by what he'd just seen. It was like a dream, it couldn't be real. He had a perfect recollection of that great bloodstain on the massive man's chest and of his rolling eyes as he slumped to the floor. He couldn't be alive, he couldn't have escaped death: nobody comes back from the world of the dead to the place where he was shot, and risks being shot again.

Vicente walked on like an automaton, as if he'd had a sudden vision and lost all awareness of the sense of things. He went down a couple of streets and decided to go into a pub. He looked for a corner at a distance from the Muzak and the chatter at the bar, and sunk a slow pint accompanied by thin cigarettes clutched between shaky fingers. This was what he'd least expected on his return to London; he'd expected it so little that he still couldn't believe it. He went to the bar for another pint, and continued deep in thought. It was all so strange: that morning he'd said goodbye to Patrick and Andy and left Trasdás, he'd caught the bus to Santiago, then the flight – and now, on the night of the very same day, here he was in a London squat with two runaway kids, and fucking Bignose was alive.

The second pint gave him the courage to decide to go into the off-licence and discover from close up whether that man was still alive. He walked there and went in. The shop assistant was gazing at a small television set and chuckling, and he continued to do so as Vicente chose some beer. He put two cans of Fosters on the counter and the bulky man turned his face, surmounted by a blue turban, with a broad smile under the huge nose and a beard tied back in strands – it really was him! Vicente fumbled with his loose change, and coins fell from his tremulous hands.

'Come on, I'll count it for you,' said the man, still chortling every few seconds at the programme, in which they spoke a language Vicente didn't understand.

The big man with the huge nose counted the coins on the counter while Vicente, in a last attempt to confirm that this was indeed the person he'd shot, took an even closer look at him. Then he picked up the money on the counter and walked to the door, his heart thundering. There could be no doubt: this was the very same man, it was as if someone were mocking him from the beyond. He opened the shop door and, as he was about to leave, he heard the shop assistant's thick voice calling:

'Wait there!'

He turned to gawp at him as his sweaty hand clung to the door handle and a sixth sense told him to run away.

'Aren't you taking the beer?'

Vicente went back to collect it and, as he walked out, he again heard the man's chuckles and the unintelligible mumbling from the television set.

13

A puff of air struck his cheeks. Curled up in the sleeping-bag, Vicente turned over as best he could. He kept his eyes closed; they were enveloped in a mist that the damp breeze was wafting over the inshore waters towards the open sea. The sky was grey, and René was running along the harbour wall with a piece of net he'd found among the boulders at the wall's tip. Vicente smiled among the long strands of hair flopping down over his forehead when he saw the little lad tug at the net caught among the boulders.

Vicente strolled along, his feet in their wet boots sinking into the damp sand. The dry sand blown by the breeze stung his face and made his teeth grate, and his hair whirled before his eyes. With Cape Sagra and Cape

O Coro keeping watch, the mist vanished over the open sea, and a receding structure of metallic lines appeared, framing the route along which the fishing boats left harbour.

He remained huddled in the sleeping-bag as his eyelashes flickered and he smelt his own breath inside it. His eyes ranged over the carpet's patterns and stains, the painted walls, the cardboard boxes piled in one corner and the dirty windows with the remains of what must have been curtains hanging at one side. He turned over and again felt the breeze; it came from a hole that had been a fireplace, ripped out and leaving the bare stone of the walls.

He remained lying there for a while as he gazed up at the ceiling. He heard noises outside and shifted his head to see the grey light slanting across the windows. Then he returned to the rhythm of his sluggish thoughts. He needed to revisit the previous day's occurrences. He was in London; but he must order the events that had led up to this damp, grey morning in this sleeping-bag. He went back over the journey in the plane, the arrival in Brixton, the argument in the squat, he'd gone into a house, found those two kids there, gone out for a stroll past the off-licence, looked in and FUCKING BIGNOSE WAS ALIVE.

When he reached this last thought he tried to spring up, as if he had a sudden cramp, but the cloth of the sleeping-bag prevented it. His limbs, stiff from the wretched night he'd spent, could hardly stir inside the bag. After trying different movements, he managed to lean his back and head against the wall and remained in this position, taking deep breaths and repeating to himself that the shop assistant was alive.

He dressed resolutely but without haste as he again tried to put his ideas in order, ideas now about what to do next. It was as if he were sitting on the edge of a razor blade with nothing to hold on to, without even a small surface on which to stand and think. The events of Trasdás and London came to mind, mingling in total temporal disorder. He must tell Patrick and Andy as soon as possible and yet, despite having seen the shop assistant alive with his own two eyes, he still couldn't quite believe it. They couldn't have been so stupid, there's a limit to human stupidity and they couldn't have ventured so brazenly beyond it. One person could be stupid but not four, or rather three: the Lizard hadn't crossed the sea because of a murder that was no such thing.

He left his room, went into the bathroom and turned the tap on, but no water came out. He heard drips in the patio; the rain was easing off, and he hurried out for some of the water running down from the roof. He pushed the conservatory door open and cupped his hands to collect water and splash it on his face. In this brusque awakening he saw the garden overrun with weeds and the fences half broken down. He repeated the washing operation several times and went back indoors for his jacket. He listened for noises from the youngsters upstairs, but there were no signs of them; he shouted their names up the stairwell, but there was no reply.

He left through the garden, telling himself again that it wasn't a good idea to stay in that house with those kids; but it wasn't worthwhile searching for another house until he knew exactly what he was going to do. It'd take him a few days to clarify the situation and find the Lizard.

He headed for the Common to catch a bus to Brixton. It was drizzling again, and he walked with head bowed and collar raised, sinking his chin as far as he could into his chest. He got on the bus and sat on the lower deck, from where he gazed through wet windows at people as they entered and left banks and shops round Clapham Common. He paid no attention to the details of the journey to Brixton, so well known to him; he felt he'd never stopped seeing them in all the time he'd been in Trasdás.

When he reached Brixton he headed for the central library. It was an old building with a wooden floor that creaked as he crossed it. He asked a librarian where he could consult the local newspaper for the month of August.

'Do you have an approximate date? It's sorted in weeks.'

'The last week in August.'

The librarian indicated a room on the right where newspapers were kept, and told him to wait there for the material to be brought. It was his first time in the library. He approached the racks where current newspapers were kept; they were in many different languages, and after a brief search he found some in English. He sat down with *The Sun* and turned its pages as he waited.

The sofas were occupied by old men of different races reading newspapers and magazines or snoozing over them; those who hadn't arrived in time to sit on a sofa were at the tables with one eye on the newspaper and the other on the sofas in case a place there became available. It was a futile effort: most of the men were pensioners who stayed away from home during the day to save on heating, and they had all the time in the world to kill on their sofas.

A little later, a man with a white beard and glasses dangling over his chest entered the room with a pile of newspapers and walked behind the row of tables where Vicente sat. He slid his chair back and asked:

'*The South London Press*?'

The man nodded and left the newspapers with him. He calmly picked them up and scanned every front page. The murder of a shop assistant in an off-licence had to be front-page copy for *The South London Press*. But after perusing all the issues he'd found no such news on any front page. Instead there was: a man in front of a burnt-down house, pointing accusingly at his neighbours' house; a face covered with knife-slashes and underneath 'Who Did This?'; the council's project for the regeneration of Brixton; shots fired in Electric Avenue; and so on.

He made ready to examine the inside pages. Something had happened that day in the off-licence: whether a man had died or not, two shots had been fired, and *The South London Press* couldn't have squandered a chance like that to dream up a sensational headline. He looked through the pages of local news, and little by little he lost all hopes of finding anything. It was as if reality, memory, dream, illusion were deceiving him and making him believe something he couldn't believe:

that day's events were things of the imagination, the incident that had made them leave London, travel by night to Portsmouth and cross the sea to Galicia had only happened in their heads.

With just two newspapers left, he spotted a small photo of the Sikh shop assistant with the big nose. There he was in his off-licence, opening the door and grinning, and under the photo were the words 'Bobha Clobbers Robbers'. A short report said: 'Bobha Singh, tired of robberies in his off-licence, has devised a dodge that makes even the canniest thieves take to their heels. By pressing a button he lights the fuses on two bangers and at the same time he squeezes a bag of ketchup under his arm, to fake being shot. On the night of Tuesday 28th August he had the chance to put his trick into practice when four thieves, three white and one black, entered his shop to steal his takings. While one of them was pointing a pistol at him, Bobha lit the bangers and collapsed with the ketchup-stain over his chest; the thieves ran away, terrified by the crime they had not committed. But Bobha confesses it was a traumatic experience and, despite the trick's success, he does not intend to repeat it. "It's too risky, it makes the crooks jittery, and they might really shoot – it isn't worth it. I got away with it this time, but I shan't try again, I'll go back to traditional methods and let the police do their job."'

As Vicente finished reading the report he heard a snigger in a corner of the room, and then it was as if all the mouths in there had exploded into simultaneous guffaws that enveloped him. Again he looked at the photo in the newspaper and felt all those stares drilling into him, leaving him half-senseless. During these moments his temples pressed in on him and his ears were filled with murmurs and deafening cackles.

He slid his chair back and eyed the newspaper from a distance with his arms crossed. It seemed to be the library's rush hour, full of pensioners in overcoats, scarves and hats, crammed round the tables and rooting in the newspaper racks. He remained as he was for a while, digesting the news. The men near him glanced beneath their raised spectacles at the grim appearance of this bewildered young man.

Eventually he stood up, gathered the newspapers together, went to the librarian's desk and asked where he could make photocopies. He went up to the next floor and made several copies of the article and the photograph, intending to send one to Patrick and Andy and retain others to keep assuring himself that what he'd read was true. A kind of fog enveloped his thoughts and actions. He returned the newspapers, and the librarian asked him if anything was wrong.

'No, no. Nothing wrong,' Vicente said, and rubbed his forehead.

He trudged out of the library, his hands in his jacket pockets to make sure that his precious discovery was still there. He felt sudden cold air strike his face, but the drizzle had disappeared. In its place was that invisible dampness that seems to rise from the ground. There were groups of the homeless seated on the stone benches in the small garden in front of the library. Two police cars raced up Brixton Hill, sirens blaring. He walked on.

He realised he'd had nothing to eat since waking up. He paused for a moment to decide whether to go to one of the cafés in the market street or to the Veracruz, a little further up, across Brixton Hill. It was Portuguese, like the Stockwell cafés, very Portuguese, yet it offered English breakfasts and sandwiches. He considered that he fully deserved an English breakfast, and perhaps it would help him gather strength to emerge from this half-dream, this fog, this uncertainty in which he was entangled, preventing him from seeing things in all their clarity.

As he devoured the sausages, bacon, hash browns, egg and toast he went over the loose ends still to be tied up. He needed to locate the Lizard, who would have sought refuge in East London, unless he'd realised that no crime had been committed and had decided to stay in South London. In any case, even though the shop assistant hadn't died, it was still an armed robbery, and that sent you down for a good few years. But if the Lizard knew the shop assistant hadn't died, why hadn't he left a message in his brother's workshop, as Vicente had instructed him when they'd parted near Reddy's house? He'd phoned the Lizard's brother several times without being given any relevant news.

He still didn't know, either, whether Reddy had discovered that he was the man who'd broken into his house and stolen his money on the night they'd fled. The events of that night remained rather confused. Reddy's lover, or his lover of two months ago at least, saw him but, to judge from the bedroom laughter that

Vicente heard afterwards, appeared not to have told Reddy anything. Vicente wondered about the extent of her loyalty. After all, wasn't she doing what he'd done – taking the Irishman's money? But what did she gain by not saying anything? Perhaps it was her secret vengeance for the way he treated her. Vicente wasn't sure what he could do to discover whether Reddy suspected him. His sudden departure, without saying goodbye, and the fact that he knew where the money was kept, were two clues casting suspicion on him. All he could think of doing was keeping a watch near Reddy's house and trying to talk to his lover, if he saw her alone. What about Jane? Better not think about Jane. It wasn't that he didn't care about her, but the effort of finding excuses and weaving a good dense net of half-truths and half-lies to try to persuade her to heed him seemed excessive at that time. His first jobs were to persuade the others to come back, search out a decent house to live in, and find the Lizard.

When he'd finished his breakfast he ordered an espresso and smoked a cigarette, with his mind now in better order and determination in his look, fixed on the door. He paid and left the café as others entered: office-workers, for sandwiches, and a few people who hadn't yet gone to bed, for a nice cup of tea. He had the phone number of Chucho's bar on him, he'd leave him a message for the others. He entered a call office in Coldharbour Lane and phoned Chucho.

'Hullo, Chucho – it's me, Vicente.'

'Hullo! The Englishman!' came down the line, to Vicente's annoyance.

'Yes, me. Look, I want you to tell my friends to be by the phone at seven, before the class begins – I'm going to call them.'

'Right. What's the weather like over there? Never stops raining here.'

'Same here. Must go now, people are waiting. Remember to tell them.'

'Right, right, goodbye for now.'

Vicente paid and went for a stroll round the market. He had several hours before him until he phoned the others, and he couldn't think of much to do. He didn't want to be drinking cups of coffee all day long, he needed to be careful with his money. He'd had to pay his airfare, and just a few pounds were left from what he'd made from the performances along the Trasdás coast; there weren't many ways to make those pounds last, and he'd forfeited his dole money and the jobs he used to do for the Irishman. If he went back on the dole it would take a month at least to receive the first cheque; and he'd have to wait until he found somewhere to give as his permanent address, because he didn't intend to stay long in that house with those kids. The house itself wasn't too bad, and if the kids left they could easily sort it out among the four of them. But the kids were there, and they weren't going to chuck them out.

He could go to the market in Vauxhall, where lorries arrived with fruit and vegetables, and retailers went to supply the South London markets. Boxes of vegetables and fruit that weren't fit to be sold to the public were dumped there, some because it had gone off or been spoilt during the journey, but much had only been cut or knocked about. You could find good food there to last several days. But then he remembered that he had nothing in the squat to cook with: no pots or pans, no cooker, no plates.

There were many ways to acquire such things for a few pence, but this needed time, and it'd be better to do it with the others' help. The best solution would be to go back to the old squat: there they had everything necessary for daily life. Now that he knew nobody had been killed, there was no reason not to go back there. The fuzz wouldn't keep watch on the house for three months, no murder having been committed. Perhaps they'd followed their tracks to the squat, but going after murderers isn't the same as going after idiots – that's what they must be in the eyes of the Brixton police. And yet there was something inside him telling him not to go back. It could only bring bad luck. The fuzz might have asked the neighbours to tell them if the squatters returned. It wasn't a good idea to become over-confident, however true it was that the shop assistant was alive.

In spite of all these thoughts, Vicente was walking, unawares, towards the old squat. Acre Lane was an important road from Brixton to Clapham; to go to Stockwell you turned off to the right. He went along Acre Lane and looked into second-hand shops to see if he could find something absolutely necessary at a ridiculous price. When he reached Marietta Road, which led to the street where the old squat stood, he came to a sudden halt and decided it was too risky to go there by day. Maybe by night, or maybe it would be better to wait and see if he could find the Lizard first, in case he knew something. It wasn't worth his while to risk everything for a few pots and pans that perhaps weren't even there.

At about two o'clock the lorry-drivers were dumping in the Vauxhall market everything that couldn't be sold. Groups of people were waiting there to be admitted: hippies and crusties on bicycles, fat women with thin, pallid children. Vicente waited with them. Once they were let in, he grabbed an empty box and filled it with oranges, bananas, mangos, apples and pears; he also put in some cauliflowers from which dirt needed to be scraped off in places, potatoes, turnips and a cabbage.

The return bus was packed and there was nowhere to sit. Vicente put his box in the place reserved for parcels and push-chairs. He was pleased with it: the youngsters would have some vitamins to gnaw on for a few days. He only thought about them from time to time, as both pitiful and a nuisance, people who are in your way. But if they really were such a problem, Vicente could soon rid himself of it: he just had to look for another house, it wouldn't be so difficult to find one. Maybe it was the knowledge that he could leave them whenever he wanted that allowed him to feel sorry for them and try to give them some small comfort, even if only for a few days. Take them fruit, feed them, keep them company, provide security – for a few days. But he knew it couldn't last, those kids had 'problem' written all over their foreheads, and when the others returned they'd have to find a place of their own.

He entered the squat to the creak of the conservatory door. Much had to be done to make this place habitable. It was clear that those kids didn't know how to occupy a house: the first thing they should have done was to put a lock on the front door and not enter every day round the back like burglars. But he didn't want to impose any changes: perhaps that was precisely their idea, leave the house as if it were still unoccupied so nobody knew it was a squat. They were about twelve years old, he'd say, but he was aware that children like these, undernourished runaways with chronic diseases, could be deceptive as to age. Kids who perhaps didn't know what affection was, a hand rocking your cradle at night, kids who only knew insults and threats. Vicente didn't dare guess their age: he knew, before he tried, that he was wrong.

He tore a piece from the cardboard box and, using it as a tray, placed fruit upon it. He went upstairs and called out to them, but their door was shut and there was no answer. He left the fruit by their door, went down to his room and saw a bag in the middle of it. He looked into the bag and found a packet of biscuits, fruit, bread, butter and jam. He smiled as he opened the packet of biscuits. He ate a chocolate biscuit and put the bag in a corner. He rested a leg on the window-frame and, as he rolled a cigarette, he gazed out at the wet street and the few passers-by. He wondered how he was going to explain this situation to his friends. The news that the Sikh was alive was the most important thing, but it'd be better to wait a few days before reaching a decision: in this matter only the Lizard could help, perhaps he knew how the investigation had gone. Maybe their tracks hadn't even been followed to the squat.

When Vicente went back to the call office, he had to join a queue. From the booths a multiplicity of languages emerged, sent to the most varied spots on the planet. Recent arrivals who hadn't yet found a way to acquire a telephone: the first thing they did once they had some money was to buy a shiny leather jacket. In the haircuts and shirts of their places of origin. Rough, harsh accents and clashing colours. Little by little they'd alter their haircuts, learn English idioms, change the colours of their clothes and, as this happened, the phone calls would become more and more sporadic until all these people vanished into the great city's anthropophagous mouth.

Standing there, surrounded by recently arrived immigrants, Vicente experienced a strange sensation. As he gazed at those mouths behind the windows of the booths, he saw the polite, worried son, the pleasure-seeker, the despotic husband, the woman whose mother is dying, the mendacious go-getter, the homosexual who has found his freedom, the reprobate lying about how well everything is going, Mister Gold Bracelets with a woman on his arm telling his wife he can't return because things aren't going at all well, the thrifty man sending kisses to his son and saying the paperwork's almost sorted. Vicente asked himself what he was doing there and which of those men was him.

At last his turn came, it was five past six, past seven in Galicia: they'd be in class by now, Vicente thought as he dialled the number.

'Chucho, it's me, the Englishman.'

'Oh, hullo, how's the weather?'

'Fucking awful,' said Vicente, acting grumpy to be rid of him.

'Hey, your voice is really clear, it's as if you were right here.'

'Can you call my friends?'

'It's what I was about to tell you, they haven't come to the class today, seems they're rehearsing, and I couldn't give them the message,' Chucho said, and replied 'Coming' to a customer.

'What do you mean, rehearsing?'

'Well I don't know I'm sure – I think they've a lot to do for a performance this weekend.'

'A performance this weekend?'

'Yes, man, yes, the weekend show.' Vicente heard Chucho yelling 'Coming, for fuck's sake, coming – can't you see I'm on the phone, a long-distance call?' He continued, 'All well there? Raining?'

'Yes, raining. Listen – is Loló there?'

'She's taking her class. Want me to go for her?

'Yes please.'

The voices from the other booths penetrated the thin walls that divided them from each other. Everybody was shouting to overcome this background noise, which made it all the louder, so that everybody had to shout even louder.

'Loló,' said Vicente curtly.

'Vicentiño!'

'What's all this about a performance this weekend?'

'Well, yes. They aren't exactly rolling in money, I'd say, don't you think? Nelo's going to help them out.'

'You can tell them we need to talk without delay. They must be there, in Chucho's bar, tomorrow at the same time.'

‘Right, I’ll be sure to tell them. Anything else?’

‘No, that’s all – tell them it’s really urgent.’

‘All well over there?’

‘All well. Raining.’

Vicente left the telephone booth with red ears and dishevelled hair. He walked in no fixed direction under the drizzle. Cars sped through puddles, splashing passers-by. Shouts and laughs rang out in the takeaways he left behind him.

14

Vicente hurried along the wet pavement of Acre Lane towards the unemployment office. He'd got up later than intended. His hair was taking on the sheen of the invisible droplets of morning mist, and this dampness mitigated the heat flowing out through all the pores of his skin. It was the heat of undigested alcohol, beer forced down the gullet, swigs gulped in the melancholy of the squat. Alcohol was sometimes the best way not to feel time or space, to be unaware of what was happening and what might happen.

His footsteps were directed towards a possibility: that the Lizard might go for his dole money. Vicente had performed all the pertinent mental operations and calculations concerning the feasibility of this event.

He knew this was the week for the Lizard to collect it, so long as he hadn't stopped going as a consequence of a move to East London, or just from fear that the police might catch up with him. Vicente knew from *The South London Press* precisely when they'd attempted the robbery, and he remembered that the next day was when the Lizard had to go for his dole: he himself had said so, this was why he'd asked for money and gone with him to Reddy's house. Vicente had counted the fortnights since then, and today was the day. If the Lizard hadn't stopped claiming the dole he'd turn up, this was at least a possibility and it had to be looked into. If he hadn't shown up for just one week he wouldn't have lost his right to it: this only happened if after more than a week you hadn't appeared at the office with a good excuse. And in the Brixton unemployment office any excuse was good. The clerks there had to face up to all sorts of stories, threats and people, and a moment seemed to have come when they'd given up for good. So the Lizard had had a week to find out how things stood, and if he'd seen there weren't any complications with the police he'd still be picking up his dole. Nerve was needed, but the Lizard had plenty of that. He was inseparable from his dole, like a limpet from its rock – he regarded it as his birthright. It was only sixty pounds a week, but they were his sixty pounds.

The other possibility was that the Lizard had gone to the East End and done his best to vanish there, never again to be seen in South London. If this was what had happened, Vicente wouldn't know where to begin. London was divided into areas that ended up as territories. East London was for him a geographical hole that felt inhospitable even before he went there. He didn't have any contacts to tell him where to begin to look. He preferred to leave this eventuality till last.

He was preparing himself mentally for the possibility of having to wait all morning near the unemployment office, and he couldn't even be sure that the wait would be fruitful. As he dawdled along, eyeing shop windows and sheltering in shop doorways, he looked for a place where he could loiter.

He stopped by an electrical appliances shop directly opposite the unemployment office. He glanced without interest at the microwave ovens interspersed with television sets, mobile phones and video recorders; behind him he could hear the engines of the cars snorting along Acre Lane and leaving an instant of speed reflected in the shop window. Higher up he saw television screens and on one of them he spotted himself. He stood for a moment gazing at it, and he made various movements to try to work out the angle from which the shot was being taken and hence where the camera was. But the images only lasted a few seconds, and they switched from one screen to another without any apparent order in their rotation. Images of the space in front of the shop window appeared at the same time as others from inside the shop, and different shots of the street. On one screen he glimpsed an image that drew his attention, but he couldn't make out what it was, because it vanished in a flash and in its place he himself appeared, seen from above. He made a quick search for that image on the other screens, but there was no trace of it. Uncertain what it was he'd glimpsed, he hastened from the shop doorway with the feeling that it might have been the Lizard.

He ran across the road, startled by the hooter of a car that had to brake hard, and hurried to the entrance of the employment office, from where he peered in. He came back out and looked down the side-street. In the distance he saw a figure resembling the Lizard: the same height and the same walk, it could well be the image that had caused his reaction. Before shouting or running towards this figure, Vicente wanted to make sure it really was the Lizard and not his own imagination combining with his hangover to project a human mirage on to a pavement near Acre Lane.

He quickened his pace and saw the figure stop at a crossroads and turn left. No more than thirty yards separated them. He saw the man in profile, and now he seemed even more like the Lizard. When Vicente reached the crossroads he stopped to catch his breath and wait for cars to pass, and the man entered one of them. Added to the futility of shouting amid the din of the traffic, there was another reason for staying silent: the car was like one of Reddy's, a white Mercedes convertible.

Stunned, Vicente leant on a pillar-box, his eyes fastened on the street down which the car had disappeared. He had driven that car. Maybe it wasn't Reddy's but a similar one; maybe it wasn't the Lizard. He was pretty sure it was, though, in both cases, but for the moment he couldn't find any explanation that would link the two facts.

Vicente sensed a gaze fastened on the back of his head and gesticulation near him, but from the depths of his astonishment he paid no attention. The movements continued, as did the gaze. He noticed a little woman with a red face wrapped in a check hood standing beside him, moving her arms in sign language and waving a hand of playing cards in his face. Vicente opened his eyes wide, shut them and moved aside so that the deaf woman could do her fortune-telling. He gazed at her performance as if recovering from shock, and then crossed the road to where the car had stopped.

His movements now were sluggish and heavy. The Lizard had stood here, his friend the Lizard – it was him, there couldn't be any doubt. Vicente's thoughts were flagging, too. He perched on the windowsill of a shop that had closed, opposite where that car had stood.

He hadn't yet absorbed what he'd just witnessed. The Lizard in one of Reddy's cars. If Vicente were doing a jigsaw puzzle, this piece wouldn't have belonged to it – it would have come from a different puzzle, it wouldn't have been one of the pieces he was looking for. In the end he got to his feet, unsure of which direction to take. He plodded towards the centre of Brixton and roamed about for a while until he ended up in a café in one of the market's less busy streets, sipping a cup of coffee. He sat at a table and gazed through the window at the stallholders and their customers as they made their purchases.

The coffee and cigarettes weren't helping him out of the fog in which he was engulfed. He felt a malaise of both body and mind from sleeping and eating badly for several days, from not washing, and from not knowing what he was doing or where he was. His thoughts kept twining together. He gazed again at the people by the market stalls, and even at the individual behind the counter. They all exuded lines of reality and defined contours – he imagined them as people who get up after a good night's sleep, shave, have their breakfast and head off for a given place where they know what they have to do. They have something to lean on while they contemplate that place, even if just the certainty of knowing where they're going. Vicente neither knew where he was looking nor where he was. It was as if behind one door there were another door, and behind every door only more doors that led inexorably to more doors.

He felt hands slapping his cheeks and water running over his head and face. He opened his eyes and the waiter was standing before him with a sponge in one hand and a concerned expression on his face. Vicente managed to keep his head upright as he rubbed his eyes and stared at the waiter in astonishment.

'You are OK?' the man asked in his broken English.

Vicente nodded and looked at the table before him. His coffee had spilt over the white plastic surface and soiled his jacket sleeves. He tottered to his feet, rubbed his eyes again, and thanked the waiter.

'Take little rest until feel better.'

'Thanks, I'm all right,' Vicente said, patting the back of the waiter who had revived him from his faint and was still directing a worried look at him.

It was like an awakening from a long dream of tunnels and farewells. The water trickling down his face gave him a sudden sense of assurance. He needed to shut himself away somewhere and think again about his situation and what he was to do. He also needed to take a warm bath, eat something decent and have a rest; but above all else he needed a warm bath complete with foam.

The only possibility that came to mind was the old squat. The Lizard had the self-confidence and the bottle to go about the manor as if nothing had happened, so there was no reason for Vicente not to do the same. In the old squat he could take a warm bath; he didn't feel safe enough to stay on and live there, but it couldn't do any harm to go and have a bath. He knew that the neighbours were out during the day.

An hour later, having collected a change of clothes, he was forcing his way into the old squat. He didn't have a key, but he knew how to open the garden window without breaking the glass. He explored the house to check its state. Entering the rooms he saw, as he'd expected, that everything of any value left behind when they'd hurried off had vanished: Patrick's radio cassette player, the television set, clothes. Someone had taken everything.

He switched the heating and hot water on, it was all working and in good order. It was hard to tell whether anyone had been living there. What was clear was that somebody had entered the house to loot it, but there were no signs that anyone had stayed there. His thoughts kept returning to the Lizard, even though he tried not to let this happen, but it was difficult not to think that the man he'd seen that morning could have been the Lizard.

He headed for the room that the Lizard had occupied, on the first floor.

He opened the door and saw that the room was empty. Not in a mess like all the others. This only meant that the Lizard had come to collect his possessions, it didn't mean that he was responsible for the theft of all the stuff in the other rooms. It only meant that he'd had time to pick up his possessions before someone else had come later to ransack the place. Vicente didn't want to impute everything to the Lizard, blame him for all the suspicious things he was coming across on his return.

He was struggling to persuade himself that there was an innocent explanation for the fact that the Lizard was using one of the Irishman's cars – because he was sure it had been the Lizard – and that everything of value in the house had disappeared without any indication that a door had been forced. He entered the bathroom and, as he pissed, he noticed a few bottles of shampoo and bars of soap left there, jumbled together, as if he and his friends were still living in the house.

After waiting in his room for the water to heat up, he went back to the bathroom and prepared the tub. He climbed in and lay there as he felt his body warm up and his pores open. He soaked the shirt he'd been wearing for two days and, stretched out in the tub, draped it over his face. Steam clouded the glass soap-shelves and filled the room like a sea mist. Vicente remained there a good while, his face covered.

He saw René running along the harbour wall and turning back, pulling faces and gesturing to wind him up. Vicente was inhaling the sea breeze as he avoided the lapping waves. He was zigzagging across the wet sand, his feet sinking into it, and then a new wave would turn a deep footprint into a few indistinct lines. He heard the roar of a motorcycle on the earth track beside the beach. It was Patrick and Andy fooling about, holding juggling props, playing with the bike, skidding it in circles. They were shouting to him to come up from the beach. They seemed to have been drinking, and were bubbling over with laughter and merriment. Vicente gestured to them to leave him be, but they kept on laughing; and now they'd parked the bike and were leaning over the wooden railings. Near René's house, on the way down to the beach from town, was a woman with a girl. He hadn't noticed them before. They were Milagritos and Carmela. They stood stock-still. The girl was leaning on her mother, and they were gazing at him as their locks flowed in the wind. He felt water in his boots and broke into a run, but the sea had already reached his ankles. He heard Patrick and Andy guffawing as he walked on and shook his trouser leg. From the harbour wall René was signalling disapproval, and Vicente could hear in the breeze: 'The sea'll get you before it gets me.' He slithered on some seaweed, he was like a gull with broken wings struggling against the wind. He looked towards Milagros and Carmela, and saw a car rolling gently down to them. It stopped and the Lizard came out. He approached them and Milagros, still gazing at Vicente, allowed herself to be embraced by the Lizard. Then one of his arms was round Carmela, too. Vicente tried to break into a run but his feet sank into the sand and the waves rose to his knees, hindering his futile attempt. Then, glancing down at his wet clothes, he realised he was dressed as Pierrot, with the flounces of his white suit stuck to his legs.

He took the shirt from his face and gave his head a shake. Then he splashed it with water to clear it. He hurried from the bath and dressed, thoughtfully eyeing the surface of the water, covered with scum and foam. The relaxation induced by the bath had dissipated in that mixture of dream and thought. He could feel gas rising in his gullet and a burning in his stomach that made him want to vomit. He rushed to the washbasin, but empty retching brought nothing up. He turned the cold water tap on and refreshed his face again. He left the bathroom half-dressed and sat in a chair isolated in what had been the sitting-room. He put his shoes on and went down to the kitchen, where there were a few plates and pans. He put them into a bag and left the house by the garden window through which he had entered.

He headed for the new squat with a strange sensation in his body. A deep, damp chill was mingling with the heat exuding from his skin. He'd always imagined rheumatism to be rather like this. Before his mother died she'd often spoken of a chill in her bones, and he'd always had to imagine what that chill in the bones meant. Now he seemed to be feeling something like what that little lady, who'd never settled into London life and had walked, head bowed and talking to herself, through the rivers of people in Portobello Market, meant by a chill in the bones. The chill that begins in your bones and goes on to squeeze your heart.

Some hours later, as he ate toast and sausages in a café on Brixton Hill, the same chill and inner feeling of dampness for which he couldn't find an explanation still held sway over him. He glanced at the clock on the wall, it was half past four; he stiffened, stood, paid and hurried out. He crossed the road and waited for one of the many buses up to Streatham.

He had the solemn, sharp face of one striving to control emotions about to burst out, as he pressed his lips together, avoided blinking, and tensed his face muscles, stretching the skin under his thick stubble. He sat by a window as the bus struggled up Brixton Hill. It passed Brixton Prison on the right and, as soon as it entered Streatham Hill, he hurried off it.

He walked a short way to the shops in the centre of Streatham, then turned right. He joined a group of people under a bus shelter; as in the morning, he was waiting for someone, or for something to happen. He was fifty yards from the travel agency where Jane worked. With fumbling fingers he rolled cigarettes in the shelter, sometimes stepping out of it to make room for people who really were waiting for a bus, and using his hand to protect his cigarette from the drizzle.

It was a few minutes to five when he saw Reddy's car, driven by the Lizard, stop in front of the agency. He saw him fiddle with the radio dial and light a cigarette. Then he tooted twice, and a female figure with her chin pressed down on to her chest walked towards the car. It was Jane. She got in, gave him a kiss, and they drove off.

Vicente felt as if something were cutting through his spine. A piece of metal inside him, ice-cold, hollow, taking up space and displacing his bodily matter. His face became even more rigid. His eyes narrowed, his lips thinned and tightened. He knew that since his arrival in London he'd been stepping on a transparent, thin, fragile tile – all there was – and suddenly the tile had disappeared from under his feet and he'd taken an involuntary step into the void. The car carrying the Lizard and Jane had dragged the tile away and left him helpless, floating on a sea of contradictory sensations. What was happening?

He thrust his hands into his raincoat pockets and squeezed their contents: a few coins, a cigarette lighter, cigarette paper, a half-empty packet of Golden Virginia. He extended his arms further, as if to stretch his raincoat, and began to walk towards Brixton, not waiting for the bus. His sharp face cut through the rain as he went at a firm pace that had never been his since his return to London. A firm pace that took him from one spot to another for two hours in no fixed direction. He remembered that he had to ring the others at seven; he still didn't know what to say. That he'd found the Lizard and hadn't spoken to him? Perhaps it would be better to wait a little longer and try to work out what was going on.

At seven he was again entering the call office, and all the faces seemed to recognise him. He was loath to look in the direction of all those pairs of eyes with their hollow sockets and withering gazes, their bulging eyebrows and thin eyebrows, their pointed jaws and leathery skin. He could walk for hours by those faces and not devote a single thought to them, not feel anything; but to see them in there as they awaited their turn or spoke inside the booths turned them into omnipresent, overbearing faces, eternal faces; they were like a collection of faces set out in display cabinets. It was as if there were just one face, presented in different ways. The skin colour changed, as did the sheen on eyes and lips and the shape of ears and hairline, but there was something that linked those faces together. All taking note, asking, and thinking about what was at the other end of the line. As if sounds, tastes, colours, smells of other markets were seeping through the phone, and these sensations were working their way into those faces and turning them into stone: harder, more pained, more stylised. They were the faces of distance. That was why Vicente was trying to hide his head between his shoulders: he didn't want to be like those faces. He didn't want that sign engraved on his forehead. He didn't want the sounds of the sea and its seaweed tastes, seeping through the telephone, to be reflected in his eyes.

He entered his booth and pondered, telephone in hand, what he was going to tell the others. He dialled and waited until a voice said:

'Hullo.' It was Chucho.

Vicente was silent for a moment as he searched for something brief to come out with, so as not to have to spend long with Chucho.

'The Englishman here. Are my friends with you? Quick – my coins are running out.'

'Here they are, waiting for you,' and he heard Chucho call the others.

'Vicente,' said Patrick.

'So I've caught up with you lot at last.'

'We're busy. We're trying to teach Nelo some tricks, and other possibilities are turning up. The fact is, we need you to come back as soon as ever you can.'

'Patrick, let's be straight about this. I came here to clear the way for all of us to come to London.'

'And can you kindly tell me which way it is that you have cleared?'

'It's something very important: you aren't going to believe it.'

'What's happened? Out with it!'

'The big Sikh's alive.'

'What?'

'Just as you heard. No shot was fired, as I've always maintained.'

'But we saw him collapse with a hand over his chest. We saw it, didn't we?'

'Yes, we saw it, but it was all staged by that sodding trickster – it was ketchup.'

'Ketchup?'

'The blood was tomato ketchup, for fuck's sake.'

'Vicente,' said Patrick, 'you're rather disturbed. Do you really think I'm going to be taken in by a story like that?'

'How else can I put it? The bastard had worked out a hoax in case of a hold-up, he'd got bangers ready and a bag of ketchup under his arm. Fuck me! I saw it in an interview in *The South London Press* and I went to the off-licence and saw the big bugger alive and kicking right by my side. Shit, what more can I say? I've got a photocopy of the interview, and tomorrow I'll send it so you can see with your own two eyes.'

A silence followed during which only breathing could be heard.

'Are you still there, Patrick?' Vicente asked.

He heard muffled words at the other end of the line and the sound of the receiver as it tangled in the lead or knocked into something.

'Are you still there, Patrick?' Vicente repeated.

'What's up?' Andy replied.

'Hullo, Andy, I've just told Patrick how things stand. Tomorrow I'll write, so you can see for yourselves.'

'Everything OK?'

'Better than expected, Patrick will explain the details.'

'Have you seen the Lizard?' Andy continued.

'Yes, no, I don't know,' Vicente stammered, loath to talk about this subject. 'I thought I'd seen him, but it turned out not to be him. I think I know how to find him, though,' he blurted.

'When are you coming back? For the time being we're muddling along with Nelo.'

'We'll talk about that later, Andy. Listen to me – I'm sorting everything out so you can come back here, OK?'

Andy took some time to reply.

'Yes, all right.'

'I'll call later, when things are clearer. I'll leave a message with Chucho when I want to talk to you.'

'That's up to you, but it'd be better for you to be thinking about coming here. We'll have time enough to go to London. Everything's going very well.'

'So that's the way things are, is it?'

'What do you mean?'

'You two don't intend to come back to London, do you?'

'No, it isn't that, but we aren't in a hurry, given the situation over there.'

'Everything's sorted. Nobody's died. Patrick will explain, and you'll see, too, in the letter I'm sending you. The guy in the offie's alive. We didn't kill him. It was all one big cock-up.'

'Are you quite sure of what you're saying?' Andy asked.

'Yes, I'm sure, and I'll send you proof in the letter so you can stick it up on your bedroom wall. I'll call again later. I'm going now.'

They said their farewells and hung up. Vicente remained in the booth for a while, leaning against the wall, taking deep breaths and rubbing his eyes, until he saw a dark face appear at the window and timid knuckles knock on it. He straightened up and walked away, leaving the shouts in the booths behind him.

15

Vicente's London days were slipping through his fingers. Silent, damp days. He felt as if he were in the middle of a dance floor and didn't know the music being played; his response had been to adopt a defensive attitude, leaving the floor and looking on from the side. He wandered from place to place trying to follow the Lizard, trying to understand what was happening. It was too soon to be angry. First he had to understand what was happening.

One day, on one of his trips between Brixton Market and the squat, he saw a car of Reddy's parked in a street and associated it with the Lizard. He hastened on, looking down at the wet pavement but casting brief sidelong glances towards the cafés and shops. He was afraid of being seen. He didn't stop to think about that empty shudder that was hollowing him out. He went still faster, and when he reached the end of the street he felt relieved.

He couldn't put into words what had scared him. It was as if he'd walked on to a stage uninvited. He pressed himself up against a wall to shelter from the rain. Perhaps it was the fear that two Vicentes might meet face-to-face and the performance shatter into a thousand broken pieces of mirror. He'd followed the Lizard these past days but hadn't taken into account the possibility that the Lizard might spot him. He was the one looking on, the spectator. He hadn't prepared himself for being on the same stage.

He gathered strength and calmed down. He glanced round, the street was almost deserted and he only saw people scurry across it from time to time, or seek the shelter of the buildings.

This street led into Stockwell Road. He went down an alley on the right towards the Portuguese café. He dragged his steps, not bothering to avoid the puddles on the pavement, and stopped a short distance from the café.

Through the window he could see the Lizard and Jane chatting and eating pastries that he immediately assumed were his favourites: custard tarts. He went to shelter in a doorway, where rain dribbled down beside him; from time to time a sudden gust blew it on to the top of his head. This impassive forbearance as a succession of raindrops fell upon him was like the way in which he was facing up to the emptying of his person. He saw the two leave the café holding hands, and head for the street where the car was parked. He remained motionless for some time, as water trickled down his face. He didn't know where to go, what to do, why he should bother to move.

Most of the afternoon he stayed in the squat, sitting cross-legged on the floor in his room, slowly digesting what had happened that morning.

It was Harlequin's master stroke. The perfect annihilation of Pierrot. Vicente had returned to London to witness his own disappearance. He took the suit he'd worn for so many performances and spread it over the floor; then he went into the kitchen for sticks and lengths of wire to rig up a hanger on which to suspend it from a nail on a wall in his room. He leant against the wall opposite and gazed at his bodiless suit, emptied of its soul, its cloth looser than ever, lacking muscles to fill it out.

Huddled in his room, he lost the notion of time; when he recovered his senses, it was evening and hardly any light came in through the window. He stood and tried to stretch his limbs as if he'd been asleep. He glanced at his suit hanging on the wall, and left the house.

He headed for a pub he'd been frequenting since his recent arrival in London. It stood away from the main streets and wasn't one of those his friends had used. It was an Irish pub with filthy old wall-to-wall carpets, and dirty ashtrays and glasses heaped on the tables. You could carry on drinking there after eleven at night, and it was often shut down by the authorities. Many Irish labourers gathered in it, phone numbers and information about jobs were exchanged, and news arrived about when the unemployment inspectors were coming after those who were working while on the dole.

Vicente hurried along and shook his limbs as if itching all over or trying to rid himself of some imaginary evil spirit that had entered his body. The damp pavements and streets gleamed under the lamps.

From outside the pub he could hear music, and when he opened the door he saw more people than usual. He ordered a pint of Guinness and looked for an unoccupied table where he could roll a cigarette. A curly-haired man with an amiable face was playing a guitar, bending a knee to the rhythm of the music as he sang old Irish ballads; he was accompanied on a synthesiser by a short, thin man with a smile that he switched from side to side. Some people were dancing: middle-aged women and men who sang to themselves as they held each other at a discreet distance.

Little by little Vicente came to life with the music, which swayed between homesickness for the distant land, love that lasts for ever, and struggles against the English. Down went the pints, one after another. It wasn't long before he joined the general merriment, clapping his hands and stamping his feet. When the doors were bolted on the inside, the party continued and he went for another pint of Guinness, drank half of it in one gulp, left it on the table and went to dance. Most of those dancing were women, some of them together, while the bar was packed with men drinking pints of Guinness who were using toothpicks to eat cockles from plastic tubs and glancing every so often at the women who were dancing.

Vicente tried to dance with various women but, with gestures or polite words, they rejected him. He didn't give up, he stayed where he was and tapped the shoulders of the women who passed from time to time. By now a couple of lads with powerful arms and glinting eyes were gesturing in his direction and casting shrewd looks at him.

Occasionally he tottered and lost the rhythm, and tried to regain it in uncoordinated whirls of limbs in disarray. He finished his pint and went to the bar for another. He noticed that some shoulders didn't budge as he edged his way through and he glimpsed surly gazes, but he wasn't prepared to be intimidated into quelling the festive excitement that had taken control of him. Some young women had joined the dancers; he took the pint back to his table, downed a mouthful and went to try his luck again. The women continued to ignore him, choosing to dance with each other rather than accept his invitation.

He grabbed at a girl with full skirts who was surrounded by other girls. She struggled to break free from his clutches, he felt hands grasping him, he heard women screaming, and both of them tumbled to the floor. A scuffle followed in which several men came and pulled him away, making threats, while others tried to protect him and prevent the brawl from deteriorating into something worse.

Eventually, after receiving several warnings, he managed to return to his table and pick up his pint. He could see a lad with broad shoulders and sullen eyes talking to the girl who'd fallen over with him. The people near his table had their backs to him. He saw the lad's curly blond head moving to the bar to join other men who were glaring at him. He rolled a cigarette with nervous fingers and noticed that he felt a little less tipsy. He sat down at the table and waited for the atmosphere to calm down. Then he went to the toilet, and while he pissed he noticed how his body swayed as he tried to aim into the urinal bowl. He went back to his table and finished his beer. He noticed that the young men with menacing eyes were no longer at the bar and, when a group of people left through the back door, this seemed to be the best time to make a move. The car park was on that side, and he could see them laughing and getting into a taxi.

He went out and felt the cool of the night filter through his clothes. After he'd gone a few yards he heard voices behind him and saw the young man with the curly blond hair, with a friend. He broke into a run and bumped into a parked car, and they ran after him.

Despite his drunkenness he managed to keep running and make their task more difficult. When they caught up with him by the railings at the head of a flight of stairs, all three paused for a moment to gasp for air. Then he heard insults and took a punch to the pit of the stomach that drove all the breath from his body and dropped him to his knees. After that, all he felt was being hoisted to his feet and, with no time even to glimpse their faces, hurled out of control on to the railings. A spectacular fall sent him tumbling down the stairs that led to the street below. He remained motionless and heard the voices of the two men as they walked away. He was injured, he knew that much even though he was drunk, but he remained as he was for a while on the cold, wet stairs as he mentally reviewed his body. He didn't think anything was broken, but he was sensible of some pains, of which he deduced that the cuts on his hands were the least serious. He knew he'd taken a hard knock on the elbow, but nothing seemed to be broken there. The upper part of one of his buttocks had hit the edge of a stair and one of his shoulders had hit the wall. Through a tear in the knee of a trouser leg some blood was visible. None of these wounds seemed important. Getting to his feet, he grasped the railings to try to keep his balance, and became aware of a pain in his left ankle. He stood still for a moment, resting against the metal rails. He descended the two remaining steps and hobbled away. There were bruises all over his body, but he was happy that he hadn't broken any bones; limping and propping himself up on walls, he headed for the squat.

16

Next morning he awoke with a dry taste in his mouth, and when he stirred inside his sleeping-bag he realised that pain awaited him in each of his limbs. He soon became aware that he'd sprained his ankle. He made bandages from strips of cloth and tied them on tight.

On subsequent days he spent most of his time indoors, to rest his ankle. Time dragged, as if the drizzle was weighing on the movement of things. In the silence of the squat he had a chance to ponder over events. He felt like a spectator at a performance, amazed, astonished.

When he couldn't stand the silence any more he'd go out, aware that he wasn't doing his ankle any favours. Sometimes he went for a stroll in Brockwell Park to see lovers canoodling on the benches and children playing on the swings, or walked to the café at the top of the park for cups of tea.

Like someone who patches up a collapsing roof with broken tiles, he was putting loose pieces of his life in place. He made his arrangements to go to the Vauxhall market for fruit, and sorted his dole money out. He was edging himself into a series of habits that formed a kind of invisible cushion on which he rested when he wasn't watching the performance that held him captive.

These last days of November, Christmas decorations had begun to appear in the streets: solitary trees among the traffic lights, weighed down with stars and fairy lanterns at which children threw stones when night came. Shops that only opened for the season, with figurines, gift wrap, Christmas trees and so on, and people who pounced on this strange prey, walking arm-in-arm under umbrellas with bags in their hands. People looked down at the ground more, and less at the eyes of other people. Nobody wanted to make friends with a stranger just before Christmas. Cold was on its way, silent and tenacious.

The children were still in the house. Between him and them a relationship of signals and hints had developed: a cardboard tray by the door, a packet of tobacco that appeared in his sleeping-bag, a strip of material for covering gaps round doors and windows that he bought for them in a second-hand shop. Sometimes he heard them leave the house early in the morning or climb the stairs in the evening. They didn't get in each other's way or ask questions. He was beginning to enjoy the awareness that the kids were upstairs: they were the only chance he had of a surprise awaiting him when he returned to the squat.

All this meant no more than a brief retreat, an aside, like the crosswords he sometimes did until well into the night, torn from discarded newspapers he came across during the day. What occupied the central place in his thoughts was the Lizard's performance. Although movement was difficult, he sometimes ventured on trips to places where the Lizard might be. It was like following a play being performed on a portable stage.

The way in which Vicente watched this enactment of his person changed as time went by. The anger and astonishment of the first days had been mixed with curiosity: how far was the man prepared to go? Perhaps, in Vicente's absence, the Lizard had simply been picking up what he'd left behind and wouldn't be able to enjoy. That would explain why he'd reached an agreement with Reddy, although Vicente couldn't understand how he could have formed a close friendship with him. It would also explain why he was trying to get off with Jane. But it would hardly explain why he took her to the Portuguese café to eat custard tarts. It mightn't have been his idea: perhaps she'd suggested it, having been there with Vicente. But the Lizard knew very well what those pastries meant for him. Vicente had explained it to his friends, though all he'd achieved was to make them laugh at him. Might the Lizard have told Jane about the meaning of the ritual? Might they have talked about him?

But later, anger and curiosity had given way to other feelings and thoughts. Vicente began to assess the

Lizard's performance. He watched out for details and compared them with the perception he had of himself. He paid attention to the Lizard's movements and gestures, and the way he walked and drove. The strange thing was that, far from feeling insulted in any way, what he felt was a sort of gratitude. His presence at this duplication of his personality was giving him a new vision of himself; this was in certain respects a privilege, one that few could enjoy. There was, however, something in the performance that he didn't find altogether convincing, and he couldn't tell whether the features he didn't like were his own, or features the Lizard had slipped into his performance, or just the way the Lizard saw him. It had been an audacious move, but this was a false audacity, the audacity and resolve of one who senses that he's being observed and seeks approval. Vicente supposed that the falseness derived from the fact that the Lizard knew he was playing a role. But who was his audience? Whose applause did he seek? Did the Lizard, the damned Lizard, Harlequin, know that Vicente, Pierrot, might be watching, judging his performance? Perhaps the Lizard was well aware that Vicente was present, viewing everything from the stalls? Perhaps he was challenging him to fight for his space.

But a little later these thoughts, too, changed: rather than judge the Lizard's behaviour as a theatrical performance, he began to view it as a displacement of his person. The dramatic features of the performance were disappearing, turning into something more shapeless and indefinable: instead of the characteristics of the action, the action itself, the act of displacement.

This new turn had plunged Vicente into a calm but turbulent sea. A sea without great waves but with deep currents. It was like floating on your back in the ocean and gazing at the clouds on high, always with that ceaseless swish in your ears, like the sound from a conch shell, the amplified sound of the ocean. Your inert body sways, part of the ocean's movements and convulsions, and your existence seems to inhabit a glass flask, fragile and transparent. Like a breath of air levitating over your still body.

Vicente knew that in due course he'd have to face up to what was happening, which would inevitably break his semi-bewitchment, this kind of magic spell; and yet there was something pleasurable and attractive in what he was feeling. He felt like an angel living an incorporeal life: as if his life were no longer real and he could pass through closed doors and live unnoticed, as if his life had departed from itself and were being lived by someone else. Something in him enjoyed this sense of unreality, the possibility that he might quietly disappear without needing to be the protagonist of the hateful ritual of death. That brutal abyss between being here and not being here. He had the chance to vanish and let another take his place. As if his body were stealing into a fog from which there was no return, and all traces of him were fading into nothingness, and on the other side of the fog he could live a different life. A life without real weight, without the weight of real existence. The life of an angel who can see without being seen.

The phone calls to his friends in Trasdás became less and less frequent. They insisted ever more vaguely that he should go back there, even offered to send him money for the airfare; with great enthusiasm they told him how the group's prospects were improving all the time, they were landing good gigs and were going to have a busy winter. The fact that the shop assistant was alive hadn't changed their attitude: for them the robbery, which they'd believed was a murder, had been a stroke of luck that had given them the chance of a new life.

Vicente limited himself to postponing his decision, stalling and saying that he was about to locate the Lizard, was trying to sort everything out; but with ever less conviction, less firmness. Patrick's and Andy's faces, and those of Loló, Milagros, Carmela, Nelo and René, were fusing into one face, their voices into one undefined voice; and they all belonged, like his sprained ankle, to that palpable, insultingly real world from which he was distancing himself by slow degrees, and which he observed with curiosity from his new life as an angel.

Even the surprising announcement that Loló was expecting Patrick's child didn't cause much of a reaction in him. He knew that something was going on between them: they suited each other. Ever since their arrival in Trasdás he'd noticed it. There was a certain communion between them that overcame the barriers of language and culture, and even that of the creatures one eats or doesn't eat. Both fought for their beliefs and believed strongly in something, and when they believed in something and fought for it they put themselves up front and accepted the consequences. He'd never had the slightest doubt that Patrick admired Loló, ever since he first saw her in charge of all before her. And Loló knew the difference between a Vicente and a Patrick. Loló had no time for Vicentes, and Vicente couldn't stand Lolós. But Patrick was different.

'I'm going to have a bagpiping son,' Patrick had declared.

'A bagpiping son? Who with?'

'Loló.'

'Who's going to teach him to play the pipes?'

'I am, when I've learnt – and all thanks to sodding Bignose.'

'And to the ketchup.'

'And to you, with all your scheming.'

Vicente chuckled during this conversation, and he was still chuckling some time later. When he left the booth to pay for the call he saw all those faces awaiting their turn, faces that had once threatened a fathomless abyss, a fall without warning, but now with bright halos and sweet, gentle features. He felt a sudden sense of fraternity: might they be angels, too?

'Good news?' a man with jet skin and African clothes asked him, beaming.

'Yes, good news.'

This good news didn't take his fixation away. He hadn't told Andy and Patrick that he'd seen the Lizard: they wouldn't understand. They wouldn't understand what was happening inside his head. It was something that belonged to him: it couldn't be shared, or understood.

Each night he returned to the house with his remembrances of what he'd seen during the day, of the places where he'd seen or hadn't seen the Lizard. Hours, perhaps, many of them fruitless, watching Reddy's house from a distance, waiting in front of the Portuguese café or the agency where Jane worked, or wandering in Tooting or on Clapham Common, it didn't matter: those dark, solitary hours when impatient tom-cats seemed to be bringing forward their rutting rituals, spiteful, menacing, fearsome. He dissected his notes, made maps, didn't know which way to turn, what to do.

On one of the first nights of December, when he came back to the squat he noticed something new. He saw decorations on the banisters: ribbons round the uprights and little coloured balls and figurines hanging from them. Surprised, he stole in, and on the landing by the kids' room stood a Christmas tree with several branches broken off. Suspended from those that remained, coloured lights glowed at brief intervals, emitting a mysterious, occasional radiance in the silence of the squat.

17

And now he was back in the Portuguese café. A levitating angel, yes, but with a human form that could scare a little girl running along the street. He continued to chew into the sweetness of the custard tart and eye his image repeated in the café's mirrors, which only confirmed his slovenly aspect, his unkempt appearance. His sore gums were enjoying the coolness of the custard. He glanced from side to side inspecting the enlarged premises, and always, always, he found a reflection of his face. The omnipresence of his face and limbs, in so many parts of the room, made him aware of his beard and dishevelled hair, his body, his human form. He even began to feel an ache in his ankle, which in recent days had seemed almost cured. He understood why the waiters were directing wary looks at him, and why the little girl he'd met as she ran and cried had sought the protection of a lamppost.

He opened one of his bags, took out the compass and the jigsaw he'd bought in the market for the youngsters and put them on the table. He shifted the compass about and watched the nervous needle as it sought north. His friends had sent him a remittance, and he'd decided to give the youngsters a present. One day his friends had asked him for the address of a post office and told him to go there to pick up some money. They'd sent a note with it, saying he was still in time to go and spend Christmas with them. He intended to phone them that afternoon to chat for a while and thank them for the money.

That cold December morning he'd got up early and done as he'd seen the pensioners do: go to the library for warmth. Then he'd taken a stroll round the market, up the back end, and found in one of the shops under the arches of the railway bridge an overcoat that would help keep the cold out, and a good scarf. He'd rooted among the boxes of ironware and found a compass and a jigsaw. He'd put his torn, dirty jacket into a bag and donned his new overcoat and scarf, also putting the compass and the jigsaw into the bag.

The memories of going with Jane to the café and other memories of former times did not torment him: they seemed very distant. It was as if they belonged to a life that was no longer his, that was being lived by another. He felt a certain relief. His resentment towards the Lizard for occupying his life, his space, had disappeared; it had been a trick of such perfection that he had no option but to acknowledge Harlequin's superior skill. It demanded his applause, an ovation from the stalls, where he, the only spectator, Pierrot, was witnessing his own annihilation.

This new state of affairs had allowed him, little by little, to shed his habits, his zigzagging. The fickle force that had once tugged him from side to side had disappeared and been replaced by a kind of peace: a restfulness that allowed him to savour this custard tart in a different way. A different sinking of the teeth into the pastry that contained the custard, an unhurried tasting, closer to the mouth and further from ritual. This calm was only possible thanks to the Lizard.

He bought half a dozen custard tarts for the youngsters – they were bound to like them. Contented, he strolled with his presents towards the squat, his neck wrapped in his raised coat-collar and his scarf. When he reached the street before the one where the squat was, he saw two ladies chatting on the corner, looking and gesturing towards it. He sauntered on, saw a third lady join them, and managed to catch a few words. They were saying something about two kids. With a strange presentiment he slackened his pace still further and, when he reached the corner, saw a police car parked in front of the squat. He stopped, and saw two policemen marching the youngsters out of the house and putting them into the car. Another police car arrived with a superior officer inside it, and one of the policemen spoke to him.

Vicente squeezed the compass in his pocket and slanted to the right across the street. Too late for the presents and the custard tarts. He walked to the Common and sat on a bench. It was cold, and the pond was covered with a thin sheet of ice. Children were lobbing stones on to it to make holes. He opened the box of tarts and ate them slowly, as if doing so on behalf of the youngsters in the hope that in their tremulous bodies inside the police car they could savour the sweetness entering his mouth. He took the jigsaw from the bag – it was of a plane soaring over a city of skyscrapers – and left it on the bench, with the compass on top.

Just as he hadn't wanted to ask or know about the kids' history, he didn't want to know how it was that the police had gone for them. It might have been something they'd done, or perhaps someone had spotted them and, realising they were under age, had informed on them. Their faces were clear in his mind, even though he'd hardly seen them after the first day; he believed he'd learnt something from that unseen relationship of objects that changed hands, objects not wrapped in gift paper and ribbons, silent objects. But it was too late now.

He realised his papers were in the squat but, fortunately, well hidden, as was his habit. It was clear, however, that the police would have realised someone else was living there, so now wasn't the time to go for them. He'd hidden them under a floorboard that couldn't easily be seen to be loose, being covered by the carpet.

As he savoured a cup of tea in a café in Clapham, he was sensible of something similar to pity or sorrow, a feeling that depressed him. He was fighting with all his strength against such feelings, because they distanced him from his resolve. Those kids, when all was said and done, belonged to the real world, the all-too-real world. They belonged to the world of wretchedness that we ignore as we live our lives; they belonged to the world that we refuse to understand. A world that was, is and will be: a world of beheaded dolls and knife-slashed dreams. He was trying to convince himself that the image he'd just seen, of policemen grasping their arms, had been lying in wait ever since that first day when he'd seen them huddled, feeble, fearful, grasping a knife later to be turned against them, in that room reeking of chemical solvents. It was an image prepared with minute care and projected with stubborn determination by a hand that has a fateful and infallible power, the power of maximum probability.

It was, perhaps, not the first time their arms had felt the firm, efficient fingers of the law, and it would probably not be the last. Somewhere in Scotland someone had entered by night while they, little children, were asleep, and had stolen their dreams: someone had chopped the legs off the rocking-horse they'd never owned. Now they were sitting in a police car, busy devising a new escape plan.

The café was filling with labourers in thick check shirts who spoke in loud voices and kept shifting their baseball caps from side to side: cigarettes between fingers, white faces and ruddy cheeks, thin lips and muscular tattooed arms. Labourers who laughed and fully deserved a good breakfast, who scraped their chairs back each time the waitress came by with a couple of steaming cups of tea or a plate loaded with sausages, baked beans and bacon, and who knew nothing about two children who'd been carted off by the cops two blocks from where they were having their breakfast. After all, what might be happening even one block away? What might be happening right here? What might be happening inside each one of them? Vicente gulped his tea down: he wanted to get out, breathe fresh air, lose himself in the streets and feel the drizzle on his face. Go out for a stroll in his new coat. He didn't want to feel the brickies' stares as they muttered to themselves or pondered in silence.

A long walk that left him on a damp bench in Brockwell Park helped him understand his situation, the fine rain on his face confronted him with the truth: he was at the mercy of the elements. Not just at that moment: he really was living his life out in the open, exposed to the damp cold of night. Wandering from bench to bench, from café to café. In a coat and scarf that had cost three pounds in a second-hand shop, all he possessed to cut a dash before the whirls of rain and wind playing at his back. This is a life emptied and taken over by another.

He'd tried all morning to prevent what had happened to the kids from changing his mood, from making him feel... what? Sad? But ever since he'd left the jigsaw on the park bench, something had been tugging at him, down below, at his trouser leg, dragging him towards a certainty that had nothing to do with the calm of the previous days. It was a sharp, cutting, ice-cold certainty that threatened to place abysses before him and made his jaw muscles ache. He couldn't feel sad for those kids, because he'd never even been able to feel love for them, he'd only related to them through signs, but mightn't being carted off by the police be perhaps their last sign? From their extreme and insulting youth and old age, from their commonsense developed by the need to find their own sustenance, from their resilience conferred by nights of fear listening to screams and screeches in the dark, weren't they making him the gift of a sign, another silent, faceless sign? Weren't they making him the gift of an exercise in wisdom? Mightn't they, too, be angels from whom somebody had stolen their souls and who were giving advice to another angel?

He went down from the top of Brockwell Park to plunge into the sea of people in Brixton Market. He strolled among the stalls covered with plastic awnings and gazed at the fishes' eyes and the Indian fishmongers talking in shouts with their customers from behind boxes of mackerel, bream, whiting, sardines and hake steaks, holding knives and wearing white coats spattered with scales. He passed spice shops with Sikhs behind the till watching the door in search of customers, with sacks of rice piled up at the back and boxes of ginger and okra by the door. He saw African cloths and turbaned podgy black mammas unrolling many-coloured textiles beneath the rain. He felt as he had when he'd gone to phone from the call office but, rather than lines of faces in display cabinets, these people resembled puppets, and the market-stalls were stages where they acted out their own stories, always appealing to the audience, shouting requests to take part in the daily celebration of the word, of life, of exchange. It was as if the figures before him had little by little been dissolving into drizzle that trickled into him and permeated him with colours and tiresome yells.

He sought refuge in the silence of a street that led out of the market area, and then decided to stroll past the squat where he'd lived with the kids, to check whether there were any signs the cops were watching. He went down a street from the Common and then along the pavement opposite the house, without stopping, even hastening his step. They'd barred the front door with crossed planks and covered the windows with formica boards. It was the sign of a squat that had been emptied.

It'd be better, he thought, to wait a few days before he went for his papers, so he headed for the squat he'd shared with the others. He entered it as easily as the previous time, and saw it was still unoccupied. Perhaps it'd been a mistake to stay in the other squat with those kids: the place he'd shared with his mates was in much better condition. But that was how things had turned out.

He switched on the heating, and tried not to be seen by the neighbours. By turning on a hotplate he found that the old cooker mended by Patrick was still working, and decided to tempt fate by staying there, a few days at least. With the strewn-about clothes that hadn't been stolen and the curtains from some of the rooms, he could fix things up so as not to feel cold at night.

On his way to phone the others he'd buy food and little things to make him feel like staying in the squat and to give himself time to consider what to do next. He wanted to break, even if just for a few days, the cycle of provisional, outdoor existence in which he'd been living since his arrival in London. For a moment he recalled the Lizard and the impersonation that had kept him so busy in recent weeks, but soon banished that memory.

He went to a supermarket and bought bread, milk, tea, biscuits, margarine, fruit and tins of beans, then went over to the drinks section for a bottle of whisky. He left, feeling tired, and dawdled on to the call office, examining the windows of the second-hand shops. He saw that in one there were some electric appliances, and went in. He couldn't see anyone in the shop, and began to rummage in boxes crammed with toasters, coffee makers, leads, plugs, screws, radios, slide projectors, taps and so on. It all seemed to have been collected from rubbish bins.

'There is more material over there at the back.' An old man's voice came from behind a pile of chairs. It was the same shop where Vicente had bought the torch on the day of his arrival.

He rooted about at the back of the shop and found more boxes of hardware.

'Are you looking for something in particular?'

'A radio.'

'You will find radios over there, I have a very good one,' the old man said, getting to his feet. He had a white beard and wore an Afghan cap. He made his way across the shop towards Vicente, pushing aside the objects in his way.

'I want a really cheap one.'

'Everything is cheap here. How much are you willing to pay?'

'A pound.'

'Goodness me, one pound?' The old man walked to the back of the shop, where he'd told Vicente to look. He returned with two radios, swaying along with one in each hand.

'Do they work?' Vicente asked.

'Well now, for one pound you can have a radio, but whether it works or not is quite another matter,' the old man said, returning to where he'd been sitting earlier. 'Come, come with me.' Vicente followed him. The old man picked up a lead fitted with a plug, and tried the radio.

'If you plug it in, it works,' he said.

He removed the lead and handed the radio to Vicente.

'One pound fifty and you have a fabulous radio, a German one.'

'All right, one pound fifty – for the radio, the lead and the plug,' said Vicente, delving into his pockets in search of the money.

'Do not take advantage of a poor old man. I could easily sell the lead and the plug alone for one pound.'

'Here you are – one pound fifty.'

'Come on – two pounds, and out you go right now,' the old man said, extending woollen-gloved hands. 'If all my customers were like you, I would be done for.'

Vicente took the radio, the lead and the plug, and stuffed them into his plastic bag. He handed two one-pound coins over and left the shop in the direction of the call office. He wanted to phone the others just to say hullo, hear their voices, so distant from all this. Then he'd return to the squat and switch the radio on: be in a house with noise, hear other voices, forget his inner voice, hear other voices. Noise and music were his idea of happiness now. Night had fallen, silent and fast, and Vicente walked on, gripping his bags, braving the rain as it struck his face. He entered the call office and requested a booth.

'Booth D,' indicated the young man behind the counter.

Vicente entered the booth and, putting his bags on the floor, sat on the stool to dial Chucho's number.

'Fuck me, Vicente, it's been quite a while.'

'Everything OK?'

'Bloody awful storm. Apart from that, fattening the capon for Christmas. Are you going to come?'

'I don't think so, I've things to do here.'

'The others are in class, better phone in half an hour.' Vicente glanced at the clock on the call-office wall and saw it was half past six, so half past seven there.

'All right. I'll phone later.'

They said their farewells, and Vicente left the booth. He paid, and decided to wait half an hour. Chucho had seemed a bit strange. Rather brusque, and surprised to be talking to him: it must have been a fortnight since he'd last called, and Chucho knew he usually called quite often. It wasn't like him not to yell to everyone in the bar that the little Englishman was on the phone, not to ask what the weather was like in England. Vicente tried not to give the matter more importance than it had, and went to smoke a cigarette in the doorway. The young man behind the counter agreed to look after his bags, and he ventured out into the night dew and smoked another cigarette, pressed up against a building. He saw two women in high heels, their legs covered by long patent-leather raincoats with slits through which their legs showed as they walked. Each had an arm round the other's waist, and they giggled as they headed for the Front Line, marked by the railway bridge over Electric Avenue. This is the line that defines the no-go area, the line not even the police cross unless their backs are well covered and they know precisely where they're going. One of these women looked like Rita, Reddy's lover. They were guffawing, unconcerned about the rain, heads bobbing up and down. Vicente felt his heart pounding. One of the women came to a sudden halt, and they both started to look for something they must have dropped.

Vicente approached them, splashing through the puddles. They were still laughing and clinging on to each other. They seemed drunk as they staggered round in circles and peered down at the ground. Then the one who resembled Rita noticed him. She looked him up and down, laughed again and pulled a face. She'd lost weight, and her features were much more prominent. Her eyes gleamed in the night with a mysterious, sickly glow. Vicente realised that Rita, like him, had begun her fall, or was well advanced on it. The gradual, relentless fall that you don't notice until it gathers speed.

'What are you looking for, this filthy night, my darling?' Rita said, struggling to hold her head upright as she hiccoughed.

'Who is this white ghost?' her friend said, lifting her eyes from the ground.

Rita stood peering at Vicente for a moment as if trying to make out the face behind the untidy beard; after looking him up and down again, she said:

'Haven't you got something to give me for keeping my trap shut?'

'Why didn't you say anything?'

'Why should I? That sod deserved to be eaten by rats,' said Rita, spitting at the ground and clutching at her friend to stay on her feet.

'What happened to you?' Vicente asked.

Rita's companion had pallid skin spattered with red blotches; two large hooped earrings hung down among her blond curls. She listened intently, pressed up against her friend.

'I wasn't as lucky as you. If he'd been robbed once, what was to stop it happening again? Kicked me out like a dog. Said he didn't like junkies – that Irish pig.' Her friend was tugging her away, but Rita slipped free and continued, 'What'll you give me for keeping mum? You've got money, haven't you?'

'Do you know anything about the Lizard, the man who drives Reddy's cars?' asked Vicente as he slid a hand into a pocket in search of money.

'He isn't called Lizard – when he's with Reddy, at least, he's Dick. Turned up at the house a few days later, I never liked him, not one little bit. He told Reddy he'd come to return some money you'd lent him. He hinted he thought Reddy'd lent it you, and since he'd no more need of it he'd come to give it back. That was how Reddy found out that you were the one who'd pinched his money. Reddy offered him a beer and they drank and chatted, and after that he kept turning up at the house. And then, I don't know, Reddy turfed me out.' Rita was gazing at Vicente's hand.

He took ten pounds out and handed them over.

'Shit, ten pounds? What a sodding waste of breath!' she yelled. 'You're the one the rats ought to eat.' She grabbed the money and, as Vicente crossed the road, he heard the crazy guffaws again. He looked back at the two women and saw they'd moved a few paces onward and were again circling in search of whatever they'd dropped.

He went back into the call office. He asked the young man for his bags and headed for a booth. When he rang, Chucho picked up the phone and handed it to Patrick, who was evidently waiting there with him.

'How are things, my little Englishman?' asked Patrick with a chuckle.

'That's all I needed, you calling me little Englishman as well. I've received the money, it's proving very useful,' said Vicente.

'We'd like you to come back. Forget the Lizard, forget London, and come back here, things are going very well.'

'When I've sorted a few matters out, I'll think about it – seriously I will,' Vicente said.

'Why not come for Christmas, and see for yourself how everything's going?' Patrick asked.

'We'll talk about it in due course.'

'Have you found the Lizard?'

'No, I don't know anything about him. He took really literally that business about disappearing from the map,' Vicente replied, brushing the question aside as fast as he could.

'Just one thing...'

'What's that?' Vicente replied.

'We've had some big storms, boats sunk and all.' Patrick spoke in grave, measured tones.

'I told you it wasn't the Costa Brava or the Costa del Sol, so don't come to me with complaints now.'

'No, I know. I'm talking about René, the lad who found us.' Patrick paused, and Vicente remained silent, with a strange feeling like the one he'd had in the morning when he was approaching the squat and heard those ladies talking about two kids.

'What did you say?' Vicente asked, breaking the silence and waiting for Patrick to reply.

'I haven't said anything yet.'

'What is it?'

'The sea got him.'

18

'That is a veritable bargain, it was the property of a real gentleman.' The little old lady – compact form, legs trotting along under her housecoat – tottered between boxes, rummaged here and there, lifted books, rugs, lamps. 'Somewhere I had one that is a little more up-to-date, and less lordly.'

'That'd be better. As you say, this one's very gentlemanly – elegant, true, but not me,' said Vicente.

'Does it need to be a suit?' The old woman turned back, hands on hips, eyeing him from the middle of the shop. Under the railway bridge, the shop had walls of bare stone and a semicircular ceiling.

'It has to be smart, but not necessarily a suit,' Vicente replied as he searched among the merchandise, not too convinced that he was going to find what he needed.

'If it doesn't need to be a suit, I have a jacket that's been worn at very high-class parties,' the old woman said, coming up to Vicente and raising a finger like someone who's just had a brilliant idea. 'I'd just need to find a pair of trousers to go with it.' Looking down at Vicente's boots, she asked, 'Do you have another pair of shoes?'

'No.'

'We shall have to see what we can do.'

She went to rummage among hangers at the back of the shop while Vicente sat on a chestnut-wood stool with turned legs. This wasn't any old junk shop, she had good-quality, well-looked-after stuff, but Vicente wasn't sure he wanted to pay good money for quality. She returned carrying a blue jacket with satin lapels and pockets. Before handing it over for him to try it on, she showed him the lining and the label.

'This was worn by an artist,' the old woman said. 'If you like it, I can let you have it at a good price.'

Vicente put it on and looked in a mirror. It was his size, a good fit. They both nodded approval.

'Not bad,' Vicente finally said, 'but it'll be hard to find matching trousers.'

'I have a pair of slim-fits, they're brand new, from a high-class shop that has ceased trading.' The old woman had a South London accent, modified and partially dissembled by a certain refinement.

'It depends how much it all comes to.'

'You're buying quality items, and I'll give you a good discount,' the old woman said. 'The jacket twenty-five pounds and the trousers ten. Such trousers – look!' From under a table she took several pairs in transparent plastic covers. 'In this establishment, as you can see, we have top-class items.'

'That's what I was worried about,' said Vicente, and took the jacket off.

The old woman muttered to herself as she rummaged among the trousers, and then approached Vicente with a few pairs to try on. She gestured to him to follow her.

'Come over here,' she said, showing him the way. 'For many years I had a shop in Balham, with a proper sign and good display-windows.' Speaking between pauses, she pointed at a curtain. 'Try the trousers on in there.'

He began to put a pair on as he heard the old woman on the other side of the curtain.

'I have dressed top people, I had very good contacts. *Forget Me Not*, that was the name of my shop, but the landlords found a way to throw me out, without any compensation, it was a tragedy. And look where I've ended up. Surrounded by blacks. I saw them coming, and ever since then everything has gone downhill.'

'It can't be as bad as all that,' Vicente replied from behind the curtain.

'How can you tell, my boy? You are too young to know. How many of us whites are left round here? You just tell me that. This used to be a good area, top people lived here. And now? They've taken everything over.'

Vicente emerged from behind the curtain with trousers that fitted him well. He went to fetch the jacket, with the old woman grumbling behind him. The trousers were tight slim-fits, the cloth was cotton, its pattern similar to Prince-of-Wales check but with lighter-coloured, smaller squares. There were short ankle slits.

'With a jersey and a pair of shoes you'll be well fitted out.'

'All right – the whole lot, shoes included, forty pounds.'

'Don't be a skinflint,' said the old woman, taking a pair of shoes on shoe-trees from a display case. 'Let me have your foot – they're Italian, you know, look here, hand-sewn, and see what soles they have.'

Five minutes later Vicente and the little old woman were beside the till taking their leave of each other, Vicente with a bag that contained a fine pair of Italian leather shoes, a good polo-neck jersey of the best wool, a jacket and trousers, all for forty-five pounds.

'Good business for both of us, don't you think?' Vicente said as he paid.

'For you, indeed. This is no place to be selling quality goods, I know that well enough,' she replied as she slipped the notes into her housecoat pocket. 'The sooner I dispose of everything and leave this place, the better.'

Vicente left the shop in a contented mood: he'd spent quite a lot of money, but he'd achieved what he wanted. He didn't want to be dressed in any old way when he confronted the Lizard. He didn't want there to be the slightest possibility that the Lizard could feel disdain for him when he looked into that man's eyes. He entered a barber's in Effra Road and watched his dishevelled hair tumble from the scissors.

'A shave, too?' the Greek barber asked as he moistened his lips and tugged on his moustache.

'Yeah, all right then.'

It wasn't yet twelve, but for Vicente it had already been the most productive day since his arrival in London. He had the sense he was getting something done, sticking to a plan, putting order into his actions. He headed for the squat: he wanted to take a bath and don the new clothes he'd acquired. On the way, he stopped at the shop where he'd bought the transistor radio the day before. He'd seen some knives in there and had decided to take one to his encounter with the Lizard. Vicente wasn't a knife man but, after brandishing a pistol and pointing it at someone's forehead, a knife was little more than a plaything. He didn't intend to use it, it was just a precautionary measure. Vicente didn't trust the Lizard and, seeing how far he'd gone in his impersonation and therefore annihilation of him, there was no telling how much further he could go or would want to go.

The decision to emerge on stage and square up to Harlequin hadn't been accompanied by any detailed thought. He couldn't imagine what kind of encounter would take place, he hadn't even considered how opportune such a move would be, or what he'd gain from it; the truth was it had much more to do with the desire to allow himself to be carried along, to bob to and fro on the waves, to let events decide and drag him with them, than with any prepared plan. Yet he was enjoying the preparation, the dressing up for the act.

It was good to feel the air on his face, bare after so long. He stroked it as he looked in the glass front of a pizzeria and smiled, well pleased with himself. It was as if his face, after disappearing more and more each day behind an unkempt beard, were now claiming its right to the light.

A little later he was climbing into a hot bath and lying calmly in it. René's grandmother came into his mind, seated on the bench outside her house, gazing at the harbour wall, where her grandson used to curse the sea. Now all her clothes were black. No joy now. Vicente thought Trasdás without René wouldn't be the same. The Trasdás he'd left so recently was no longer the same. Patrick about to have a bagpiping son, and Andy with Nelo. Loló with her Patrick, clutching him protectively. The sea without its little tyrant to probe into its wounds. Vicente hadn't been there to experience all these things, just as he hadn't seen the bridge being built, as Milagros had; nor had he been there to see the boats searching for René, or his bloated body wrapped in seaweed.

He didn't want these thoughts to torment him on a day that had begun with such decisiveness. He was preparing for the big occasion, the final act. It was like going up to a sheet of plate glass and trying to walk through it: he wasn't scared of the vertigo he might feel on the other side if he managed to get through. But perhaps what awaited him was smashing into it and being hurt, departing with bloody hands and the pieces falling at his feet. Whatever happened before that glass with his image reflected in it, he was ready. It was like gazing into his own eyes, searching for his own look, defying the magic of duplication. He was ready, and perhaps Harlequin was, too. Perhaps the Lizard had been longing for this moment. Perhaps all the Lizard's acting was directed at this climax, perhaps this was the final scene of his performance. The solving of the mystery of reflection. The hour of the lizard.

He dressed slowly, making sure his clothes sat well on him. He walked to Reddy's house and waited on the other side of the roundabout, watching from a bar stool through the red words of the menu written on a café window. It was a small café where the moustachioed Turk hurried from side to side preparing doner kebabs, sausages and chips. Vicente ate eggs and chips and saw people come and go, as the Turk sent worried glances in his direction: this wasn't a place anyone would choose for whiling the hours away. Vicente went outside every so often to stretch his legs. Just as he was about to admit defeat after his long wait, at about six, he saw the Lizard arrive in one of Reddy's cars. As Vicente had done before him, the Lizard drove the car into the garage. He knocked at the front door. Vicente saw it budge, but at that distance he couldn't see who was opening it. He felt some relief when the door closed and he knew the Lizard was inside those walls. Sooner or later he'd come back out. That would be the moment, and then there wouldn't be any longer to wait.

After half an hour a plump blonde emerged from the house. She returned a little later with a bag from the off-licence. She walked precariously on her white, high-heeled shoes. She was short and had eye-catching long hair. When she reached the door, she rummaged among her keys and went in.

Vicente waited as night fell, keeping his fingers busy with cigarettes but with an inner calm that gave him the certainty that he knew what he was doing. The abyss wasn't before him, it was behind him. This put a special sheen on his eyes, which remained impassive, seldom blinking, fastened on the front door of Reddy's house.

When he saw Reddy and the Lizard emerge, each with an arm over the other's shoulders, chuckling as they descended the stairs to the street gate, he could only marvel at the skill the Lizard displayed in his impersonation. It was clear they'd been drinking, and now they were perhaps going for the final pint before the bell was rung for last orders. He waited for them to start off. Along they strolled, stopping every so often to talk and laugh. They went up Brixton Road. There were a couple of pubs on their side of the street, one of them the place where he'd stopped to count the money on the day he'd broken into Reddy's house. But he didn't think they'd go in there: it was full of West Indians playing pool, and he knew Reddy didn't like that kind of pub. Reddy tolerated blacks only so long as they formed a certain percentage and so long as that percentage was a minority. Reddy knew there'd been a time when some pubs had had a notice on the door saying 'No blacks, no dogs, no Irish', but he was convinced the Irish were on a very superior level to the other two groups. The other pub on that side of the street was for youngsters, with live music, very noisy, and wasn't to Reddy's taste, either.

Vicente followed them at a distance of some fifty yards on the other side of the street. They turned left and he soon realised they were heading for the Small World, an Irish pub on the outskirts of Kennington. Their route took them down ill-lit side-streets. The Small World was surrounded by buildings, and there weren't many places where you could find such a discreet hidey-hole to pass unnoticed.

Vicente could see by the light of the few street-lamps that the two figures were in heated conversation. He felt uneasy, prowling in the dark like some silent cat. Since he knew where they were going, he didn't need to stay too close to them. He'd been there with Reddy several times. It was a small pub where many Irish labourers of the area met up. Young girls served at the bar, and when they poured you a pint of Guinness they drew a shamrock in the foam with the utmost care by moving the pint beneath the beer tap. There are many ways to overcome distance.

The two men entered the pub, and Vicente continued two streets further on, to an off-licence where he bought a couple of cans of beer. He didn't want to be the only one who was dry on that cold night. Then he strolled back to the pub with one can in his jacket pocket and drinking from the other. Every so often he came across someone rushing to the off-licence for their nightcap or scuttling back home. A man standing in the street for hours on end was a sorry sight and could only raise suspicions: he knew the Small World shut at eleven but let its customers stay inside drinking. He paced this way and that as if going somewhere, but he couldn't do this for long, either. In the end he resolved to go to another pub and wait there till closing time. It was almost certain that Reddy and the Lizard would make the most of the opportunity to drink more beer after the pub closed.

Vicente sat at a table with a pint. The wait was making him impatient. His idea of an encounter was limited to two bodies face to face, two glares confronting each other. But all this lying in wait and pursuing along dark streets made him feel insecure, gave him time to think, to probe among ideas, those creepers that kept tangling in his mind. Even the clasp-knife he was carrying felt awkward, it had acquired a real and strangely solid form. It was hard to root about in his pockets in search of something and not come across this lump of metal that could cut.

The encounter was acquiring tones that were different from those it had possessed before: from being a way to solve the problem of the impersonation, the performance of his person, it was acquiring a dimension that was more immediate and real, a dimension in which what mattered was the silence of his footsteps, his skilful use of opportunity, the patience of his wait. It had nothing to do with the care he'd devoted to this moment, the money he'd spent on dressing for the occasion. The limit he'd hoped to transcend, the plate glass he'd hoped to walk through, were becoming empty thoughts as he waited in the pub, raising his head every few moments towards the clock on the wall, feeling at frequent intervals for the clasp-knife in his pocket or unexpectedly coming across it.

He rolled a cigarette, his gaze fixed on the table. Seated there, he was close to the man who'd supplanted his person, occupied his spaces and left him in a kind of limbo, on a soft, flimsy surface, in aimless behaviour, stripped of his habits and inner energy. The Lizard had gifted him with weeks that had sunk him in a fog of uncertainty, a fog that had impeded his awareness of the outlines and colours of things.

Now he was a small distance and a short time away from being in a position to break the spell that was keeping him in chains and regain, if not his physical space, at least his life space. But it was this, precisely, that dispirited him as he stroked his finger round the top of his beer glass: being himself again was what he didn't find altogether attractive. Being that lost shadow zigzagging over wet sand. It was a quarter to eleven, and Vicente wished the clock would stop and give him more time to think. Little by little, like a cloud drifting over the light of the sun, the chance to see himself reflected in that glass was starting to seem like a bad omen. The place was becoming an undesirable one. What if he did break the spell and, as the pieces fell to the ground, the two figures were still clearly distinguishable? Vicente and his double. What did he have to gain by making the differences between the two clear? What did he have to gain by recuperating what he had once been and someone had snatched from him?

'Come on, pal, time to go,' the bartender said, taking the ashtray away.

Vicente stayed a little longer, smoking his cigarette and finishing his pint. And he thought: if the Lizard had supplanted him and occupied his space, what had become of the Lizard's space? Couldn't he now occupy that empty space, pick up the persona the Lizard had thrown away so as to appropriate his? Couldn't he make use of the Lizard's skills, which had enabled him to stop being what he'd once been and play a different role, as lizards shed their scales to leave room for new ones? Wasn't this the true challenge, the true glass to confront and overcome? Renounce himself for good and be reborn as something new. Allow the Lizard to enjoy what he desired, leave him with his play and performance, to await its ending. Vicente could grasp an opportunity he'd never dreamt about but now had before him, within reach. All he had to do was leave this pub and go in the opposite direction. Forget everything and enjoy his new clothes, let someone else live in the zigzag trap.

He felt for his knife to make sure it was still there, and took the last swig of his pint. He left the pub, answering the goodnights of those who remained. He headed for the pub where Reddy and the Lizard were drinking. His were the contradictory feelings of someone who has long awaited a certain moment and then finds it doesn't live up to expectation: someone who wants to relinquish what he has desired, not carry out what he has planned, but is incapable of stopping and changing course, of going elsewhere, of breaking the bonds in which he's tied, bonds that force him to carry out an action he no longer wishes to carry out.

He didn't have the slightest desire to recover his own self and put an end to the impersonation that, during those weeks in London, had astonished him more and more, as if he were witnessing his own displacement, and yet he was pacing forward, clutching a knife he didn't want to use. Was this the final act? The denouement wanted by nobody, yet apparently inevitable? If he didn't go through with it, wouldn't what awaited him be a ghost's life, wandering like the lost souls of the *Santa Compaña*?

A car drew up outside the pub. Reddy and the Lizard were talking by the open door of what must be a taxi. After a while they embraced, Reddy got in and the Lizard closed the car door. They waved to each other, and the Lizard walked in Vicente's direction, on the other side of the street. Vicente crossed over. He could make the Lizard out at that distance, staggering from drink and gazing down at the ground. He saw him take a cigarette from a packet he then threw into the street. The Lizard stood there with legs apart, searched in his pockets for his lighter, and showed his annoyance when he realised he didn't have it on him. He turned back to glare at the pub, and swore and shook a fist at it. He continued towards Vicente, who walked on with a grim look directed at the ground and his hands in his jacket pockets. When they were less than ten yards apart the Lizard swore again, with grand movements strode over to a wall and opened his flies in front of some bags of rubbish. Vicente slowed down and saw the Lizard start to piss. When he'd almost reached him he could hear his slurred voice:

'Hey, pal – got a light?'

Vicente went and stood behind him. His heart was thundering as he lit his lighter and held it out. The Lizard grasped his wrist as the piss spattered on to the bags.

'Your wrist's very shaky, pal,' the Lizard said.

'It's the night cold,' Vicente replied, disguising his voice a little.

He put the lighter back into his pocket and continued on his way, leaving the Lizard propped up against a wall, trying to zip his flies up.

19

Floor tiles gleamed and legs moved in all directions, bringing suitcases, bags and trolleys behind them. A group of Spanish tourists took a map out, opened it and proceeded to give each other directions and orders about meeting, assembling, and not getting lost. A man carrying a briefcase and wearing a pinstripe executive suit stopped beside them and stood there, glancing up again and again at the clock and the departures board, then he went into the newspaper shop and emerged with the *Financial Times* and *Le Monde*.

Groups of people were giving each other hugs near the departure queues while others were watching, cigarettes between fingers, from the Costa coffee shop. Next to some Japanese tourists stood a tall, large lady with curly, off-white hair and a red face. She was turning round and round beside a suitcase. She seemed to be questioning everyone who walked past.

'Anyone know where to go for Santiago?' she was saying in Galician, to the surprise of passers-by, which was evident in the looks they directed at her.

'Anyone know where to go for Santiago?' she kept repeating.

The lady turned this way and that, unsure whether to look at the departure boards or the people round her, waiting for someone to take her where she needed to go. After a while a firm hand tapped her shoulder. She turned, breathing hard and becoming redder and redder.

'Come with me.'

Vicente stood behind her, beckoning. The lady was all smiles as she seized her heavy suitcase as if it were a newspaper and began to talk and talk. She'd spent three months working in a relative's kitchen and had decided that enough was enough.

'They speak like dogs, my friend. I'm off home, dearie. I've had enough. You can't live in this place.'

Vicente nodded to all she said, and led her towards the departure lounge. When they reached the duty-free area he asked her to sit down. She did so with the suitcase on her thighs, and gazed at people of all races and languages as they walked by. She muttered to herself as she kept trying to see where her saviour had gone.

Vicente was in the toilet splashing water on to his face. He wet his hair, combed it back and then examined himself, dressed in his new clothes, in the full-length mirrors. Several days had gone by since his non-encounter with the Lizard, and his appearance had improved. He had a new smile on his lips, a new gleam in his eyes. He'd taken care to eat well and had had time to collect everything together, make arrangements for leaving, go for his papers to the squat where he'd stayed with the kids and wait for the others to send money for the airfare. They'd been restful days. He felt he was leaving nothing behind. Nothing to recover, to search for, to see. His image reflected on to the Lizard had proved in the end, he thought, to be his salvation. Now he was someone else. He'd been freed from himself and, thanks to the Lizard, could begin another life. He felt light. As if he'd left a great burden behind.

He picked his bag up and headed for where the lady was seated. She stood up when she saw him coming, and offered him a chocolate bar. She went on chattering happily, and Vicente pretended to listen as he glanced every so often at the departure boards. When their flight was announced they traipsed down the long corridors. They boarded the plane and took their leave of each other. The lady had the good fortune to be given a seat beside Galician emigrants who were going back home for the holidays, happy to share experiences, while Vicente went to his place at the back.

He sat down and enjoyed a pleasurable sensation as the plane took off. Every so often he replied as best he could to two English tourists' questions about routes and places to visit. But little by little he drifted into a calm sea. He began to nod off, and opposed no resistance to the summons of sleep. The tourists stopped asking questions. He stretched his legs out and slept.

20

Patrick was driving with one hand on the wheel and the other on his thigh. Vicente was poking his head out of the window to feel the cold air on his face.

For some time they'd been waiting for spring to arrive and at last it had, with a cool breeze you could feel in the early morning before it drifted away out to sea together with the damp and the clouds. It had been such a harsh winter old people said they didn't recall one like it for many a long year. René's death would remind them of it for many more years to come: a bead in the rosary of lives taken by the sea. His grandmother spent the hours seated on the stone bench by her front door staring at the harbour wall. His mother had come back from Canada to do for her mother what she hadn't done for her son.

The clowns had decided on a fortnight's rest. Without performances or rehearsals. They'd had a surprisingly successful year, and had taken their acrobatic feats and other entertainments to all corners of the coast, and even to towns and cities. They'd made contacts and had offers of collaboration with theatre groups from various places, and their own projects were under way. Andy had put his mind to work on ideas for a performance during the summer festas, on a modified mussel raft in the harbour. Loló and the people at the local secondary school were also involved, obtaining the necessary permits and organising the performance.

Halfway through winter, Vicente had begun to feel strange pains. They'd come on as he awoke in the morning, but they weren't too frequent. He tried to ignore them, and it was some time before he told the others. They'd realised something wasn't right when he couldn't rehearse a couple of times because of aching joints. After much insistence from them and Milagritos, he'd agreed to submit himself to a check-up.

'When do you have to go back?' Patrick asked.

Vicente didn't reply, and made a gesture of indifference. Patrick, surprised, glanced at him and continued driving.

'If you've had tests they'll need to give you the results.'

'I don't know. They'll phone in due course.'

Vicente turned the dial on the radio, rummaged among the cassettes and put on a tape of Latin jazz.

'How's Loló?'

'She's OK... it's all going well. No more pains, after the first few months.'

There was a pause while Patrick tackled some bends.

'She's sticking to her guns,' he said a little later.

'She doesn't want to marry?'

'I don't mind not marrying, but I would like us to live together. That's no secret. You don't get to be a father every day of your life.'

Patrick's face was grim: he was clearly affected by what he was saying. He fell silent again, and patted the steering-wheel. In the surrounding scrub stood isolated bramble-swathed shacks with graffiti on their walls. They drove on for a while without a word as Patrick took the bends slowly, sizing them up.

'There are times I want to cry,' Patrick blurted.

'Cry? What for?'

'Because I'm happy,' and saying this he giggled nervously, as if to suppress his emotions. He stretched in his seat and took deep breaths, and his eyelids flickered as he tried to conceal tears that hadn't yet emerged. Vicente slipped a little lower in his seat and, somewhat surprised by what his companion had just told him, covered his mouth to hide edgy, amazed laughter. But when he looked at Patrick, suffering as he contorted the muscles of his plump face to hold his tears back, he couldn't prevent a nervous guffaw from bursting out of his mouth.

'Don't laugh at me,' Patrick managed to say as the tears rolled down his face and he wiped them away with his free hand.

'If you weren't driving I'd give you a hug,' Vicente stammered, looking straight ahead and trying to suppress the tears that were beginning to run from his eyes, too.

When Patrick saw Vicente's watery eyes, he lost all self-control and broke out into choking sobs. He drove on a little with his head near the steering-wheel, and then decided to stop on the hard shoulder.

The two friends hugged each other as they wept and laughed, ignoring the hoots from passing cars. After a while they separated, patting each other on the back and drying their tears as they gazed through the windscreen.

'There's nothing like a man crying,' Patrick commented.

Once they'd calmed down they drove off. Cool, clean air flowed in through the windows. The frost that had covered the edges of the road when they'd driven to the hospital in the morning had disappeared. In its place were slates with a shiny, transparent surface evaporating under the sunbeams that cut through the air like arrows of light.

'You aren't getting on too badly with Milagritos, either.'

'Sometimes I want to hold her so tight I'm afraid of breaking her,' Vicente confessed as he took tobacco out and rolled a cigarette. 'Other times I wonder why I want to hold her so tight.'

Patrick eyed him with an incredulous look.

'Take care, then – you never know...'

Vicente peered at Patrick out of the corner of an eye and demanded:

'What's that: English sarcasm or Galician irony?'

'Jamaican leg-pulling... Come on, make one of those for me before you get tired.'

Vicente took his tobacco out again and rolled a cigarette.

'So we're all paired up... or perhaps I should say snared up,' Patrick remarked as he took the lighted cigarette that Vicente handed him.

'You with Loló, me with Milagritos, and Andy with Nelo...'

'Fucking hell, when we boarded the boat and said we had to go over to the other side, Andy took it really seriously,' at which point he burst into laughter. 'Remember *The Full Monty*?'

'"There's nowt as queer as folk."'

The two of them chortled.

'Sod it, I think I'll have to stop again, this time to laugh,' said Patrick, his head close to the steering-wheel once more.

When they reached the coastal road, Patrick concentrated on his driving, and took great care over the bends. He smiled whenever someone at the roadside waved to the van, which everybody recognised. Loló had let them paint clowns on it. When Vicente had arrived, there had been, much to his annoyance, a Pierrot on one side. He'd intended to paint over this character, which had vanished from their act, and cover it with other clowns, to erase that restless, melancholy being for ever. But he hadn't got round to doing so.

When they reached Trasdás, Patrick left Vicente in the middle of town and drove on to Loló's house. Vicente headed for home with the hospital papers. He came across the fish van and approached to see what was on offer. The fishmonger greeted him and called him over. She had sardines, ling, whiting, megrims and small horse mackerel.

'Two dozen horse mackerel.'

The fishmonger picked up a plastic bag, put the fish into it and held it out to Vicente; then, still holding the bag, she asked a young woman what she wanted. She asked for two whitings, and the fishmonger was surprised that Vicente had neither paid nor taken his bag. She looked round and saw him standing there with rigid arms and a grim look on his face. He was trying to straighten his fingers and move them towards the plastic bag. His hands were clenched, and he was doing his best to hide the pain of the sudden attack. She could see he was worried.

'Anything wrong, Vicente?'

'No, nothing, just cramp.'

'Take the horse mackerel, you can pay tomorrow.'

Vicente went home without the fish. With his hands thrust inside his jacket, he felt his fingers starting to relax and straighten. He managed to grasp his keys, and fumbled the front door open. In the kitchen he poured himself a glass of wine, rubbed his arms together and looked out into the square, where the fishmonger still stood beside her van, chatting with some locals.

21

Nearly summer, and the devil
Still comes visiting his poor relations.

Dylan Thomas, *The Notebook Poems 1930-1934*

The sun was falling in fury upon people's heads. Cars raised dust as they drove along the dirt road. In the pine grove there were hammocks, portable tables and folding chairs. Women in bathing costumes carried lunch boxes and laughed. Men sat with red bellies, cigars in their mouths and hands always close to glasses of sangria. In some places bags of rubbish piled up, and at the edges of the grove people queued at taps that had been installed there.

Patrick and Loló were walking through the grove carrying bags. Loló's pregnancy was far advanced, and she lurched along, hoisting her weight first on to one leg and then on to the other. Patrick plodded by her side, trying to pull bags from her hands.

'Stop it – I'm not totally useless.'

She took deep breaths, and drops of sweat ran down her forehead.

'Do you think Vicente's trouble is anything serious?'

Patrick took his time to reply as he went along at Loló's pace. Children crossed the dirt road, and adult voices warned them to be careful. A streamer of children's laughs floated between Patrick and Loló.

'I don't know what to think,' Patrick said finally. 'He only has these spasms from time to time. He doesn't like going to the doctor's...'

'Nobody likes going to the doctor's... but such things need to be seen to.'

'To be honest, the doctors aren't saying anything, either.'

'Don't make excuses for him.'

'I'm not making excuses... but they send him from one specialist to another. I'm not surprised he despairs and doesn't want to go.'

'It'd be better for him to be properly checked out now – before it's too late,' Loló said, and stopped to rest for a moment.

They spotted Milagritos in a swimsuit, between the beach and the pine grove, waving both arms.

'There they are,' said Patrick.

The couple continued towards Milagritos. Andy went to help them, leaping among the pine trees to avoid the brambles. The three friends soon reached the edge of the beach. Loló remained in the shade while the other two strolled towards the towels. Vicente waved to Loló and she waved back as she sweated and tried to find a better position.

'We've brought the sardines and the drinks.'

'We've brought omelettes. Come on, Vicentiño, weren't you supposed to be in charge of the barbecue?' said Milagros.

Vicente was on the sand playing with Carmela, using a spade and a bucket to make a canal. He took his T-shirt off and began to excavate a tunnel.

'Oh, how horrid!' Carmela screamed.

'What's up?' Milagritos asked.

'Ugh!' the girl exclaimed as she jumped to her feet and clung to her mother. She was pointing at Vicente's back.

'That's no reason to get into such a state,' Milagritos replied. 'He's peeling. It's normal. When people stay out in the sun too long their skin gets burnt and it peels.'

'That isn't skin,' Carmela cried, and pointed at Vicente's back again.

'What do you mean, it isn't skin?' Milagros asked. 'What else can it be, Carmela?'

'It's scales.'

'How can you say such a thing?' Milagros retorted as she went to Vicente's side and ran a hand over his back.

Then she was silent for a moment, rubbing her hands together and peering at his back. She commented:

‘To tell the truth, Vicentiño, you do have very strange skin. I’ve never seen anyone’s skin peel like that. You must take care.’

They heard Patrick’s voice as he took soft drinks from a cool bag:

‘Come on – are those sardines going to barbecue themselves?’

There was a festa in one of the villages along the coast, and a solitary sky-rocket resonated every so often. Vicente, kneeling in the sand, lifted his gaze towards the glare of the sun, high in the sky like a palm tree in an eruption of incandescence; then he ran his eyes over the area between the pine grove and the beach, where there were gaps between the stones. Rockets were bursting in the distant sky at ever more frequent intervals, with delayed, sharp sounds. Vicente felt an immense urge to scurry over to the crevices between those stones and seek shelter there. A battery of rockets exploded with the sound of wooden seats being snapped shut in a theatre.

Read more fiction in English from Small Stations Press:

Xelís DE TORO, FERAL RIVER

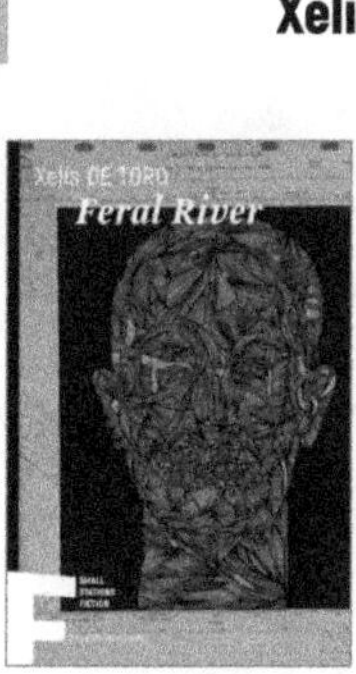

A boat with the charred body of a man crucified on its mast turns up at the mouth of the river in Romero, a town on the frontier. The boat belongs to the owner of the printing-firm that publishes the local newspaper. He engages Marqués, who is from the east coast and claims that he can write, to head upriver to find out the causes of the boatman's death. His only deckhand is a mestizo boy called Cordel who's learned his trade from the previous boatman ('What you steer isn't the boat, it's the river'). They soon reach the mission, which is staffed by a single friar, Father Bento ('He seemed to chew his words like a cow chewing grass before releasing them in short bursts'). The friar asks if Marqués has come to judge, to govern or to execute. 'To tell,' is his answer, 'I'm a writer.' Marqués, however, soon falls into a fever and has to be cured by the healing-woman from the local Aventurei Indian tribe. He realises that entering the world of the river is like clambering up a liquid wall on which there are no ledges or crannies for hands and feet to cling to. There is an obvious parallel between this narrative and Joseph Conrad's *Heart of Darkness*, in which the journey is an end in itself and the reader doesn't know what secrets the river will reveal. There is also the writer's own personal journey in search of fulfilment through his art. Marqués and Cordel will be joined on board by Rufus the Strongman and Ela, circus workers, as they struggle to come to grips with the tangle, both real and imagined, of the jungle.

ISBN 978-954-384-105-9

Fran ALONSO, NOBODY

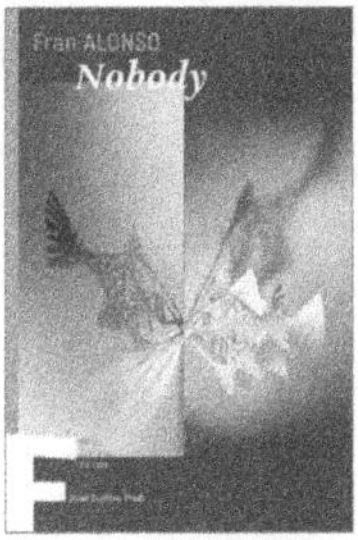

Nobody by contemporary Galician writer Fran Alonso is a book of ten short stories about noise (and silence), the disjunction in our lives between what we really feel and our public persona. In these stories, a man is bombarded by the noise from his neighbours and goes upstairs to have it out with the woman who is always shouting at her children, with unforeseen consequences. An Old Man lives in a semi-deserted city; his only way to mark the passing of time is to make a cut in his hand every day – that is, until he spots an Old Woman on the balcony opposite who is constantly knitting. Sick and tired of noise in the city, a woman endeavours to change her lifestyle by moving to a house on a cliff. Writer finishes a novel and leaves it on a lectern in the lobby for his neighbours to read. S. Lonely, who relies heavily on technological gadgets to keep himself entertained and prefers not to go outside, is so bored during the holidays that he decides to go on a trip... Every story in this book analyzes the relationship between the individual and society, the individualism of urban living versus the community obligations of the village, forcing the reader to reconsider the kind of world they live in and the sincerity of their relationships. This is a book for our times that draws on the powerful story-telling tradition of Galician literature.

ISBN 978-954-384-124-0

Susana SANCHES ARINS, and they say

and they say is a dazzling piece of writing by contemporary galician writer susana sanches arins. suffering is a black stormcloud on a sunny day. the trouble with remembering is it can cause damage. but it can also heal. the translator of this book, the north american professor kathleen march, suggests that and they say (seique in the original galician) is its own genre and what really matters is telling (recovering) the truth. it is a story of betrayal, unspeakable cruelty, and the odd (breathless) act of compassion. it is the recuperation of the collective memory of the spanish civil war (1936-39) and its aftermath, when fugitives were caught and bodies thrown into ditches, when it was dangerous to answer your door at night. it is an essay that records testimonies, acknowledged and anonymous, of some of the dark nights that characterize this period of spanish history. it is poetic (if poetry can be cruel). it is also tragic, down to the repeated appearance of the chorus, which seems to reflect on, to reinforce, the central message: memory can be painful, but it is best acknowledged, so that the mourning can take place and the survivors can move on. this book, expertly collated, is a masterpiece of writing on the spanish civil war, an essential piece in the puzzle of those years.

ISBN 978-954-384-123-3

For an up-to-date list of our publications, please visit www.smallstations.com

CPSIA information can be obtained
at www.ICGtesting.com
Printed in the USA
LVHW110551080622
720767LV00001B/118

9 789543 841288